TAINTED LOVE

Soho Noir #1

T.S. Hunter

RED DOG
UK

Published by RED DOG PRESS 2019

This work was Edited by Eleanor Abraham

ISBN 978-1-9164262-6-9

www.reddogpress.co.uk

For all those who came before, who fought for us to have what we have now. Thank you.

1.

SOHO, LONDON. 1985.

THE DANK WINTERY STREETS outside were a distant memory now. Tonight, this hot, sweaty, neon-lit club was Joe's whole universe. Music pulsed through his body like a brand new heartbeat. London was already changing him.

Sweat sticking his T-shirt to his ribs, arms raised high above his head, grinning wildly, hips pumping to Frankie's repetitive call to "Relax". Joe hardly recognised himself and he was happier than he'd ever been.

It had been a night of Bronski Beat, Sister Sledge, Culture Club and Madonna—the kind of upbeat pop Joe usually hated. He was into more brooding, melancholic stuff—*miserable shite*, according to his friend Chris—and yet these pulsing, happy beats felt like they defined him right now. The new him. His new start.

This whole weekend had been like none Joe had ever known. He'd always been the quiet one, never even daring to come down to London on his own. Not confident enough to admit who he really was. This year was different already.

His oldest friend from school, Chris Sexton, had called him out of the blue to invite Joe to join him in London for a long weekend. "A friend is having a party," he'd said. "It's going to be wild. You should come."

Chris had been the only person Joe had stayed in touch with from his school days. His first and only love, though he knew that particular accolade was one-sided, and Joe had long since given up hope of anything happening between them, even if he was still— and always would be—a little besotted with Chris.

Chris wasn't the kind of guy who went around falling in love, though. Handsome, confident, reckless, funny and the bravest man Joe knew—Chris had left a trail of broken hearts behind him of those who'd fallen for him before they realised he'd never settle down.

So Joe and Chris had stayed friends, meeting up less frequently now that they had both left their respective universities, and Joe had secured a boring but well-paid job with the council back in their old home town.

Chris, on the other hand, had moved to London seven years ago to study fashion at St Martin's College. Two fingers up to his father, who'd wanted him to join the family accountancy firm. Maybe he'd go back to it when he'd settled down a bit. Though there was no sign of that happening any time soon.

After college, Chris had hooked himself up in a partnership with a couple of other young designers, and had been making a name for himself on the fashion scene ever since.

He was renting a flat in the heart of Soho and seemed to have a wide circle of friends of all shapes and ages. Joe wished he had Chris's life. Or his talent. Or his looks. Any one of those would do.

Joe laughed as his friend bounced across the floor in a series of typically ostentatious dance moves, deliberately bumping into a tall, skinny, blonde guy—exactly Chris's type—and planting a sly kiss on his cheek before sashaying away again. *Oh, for that confidence.*

Joe hadn't even come out to his family yet. In fact, Chris was the only person he'd ever confided in, though he was sure others knew.

TAINTED LOVE

His oldest sister suspected. She'd asked him outright once, but he'd just changed the subject. It was none of her business. She was like the mirror of their mother. She wouldn't understand. She would just worry.

All of that felt a lifetime away right now. Here in this club, Joe had found his spiritual home. This was living. This was who he really was. "Like a Virgin" by Madonna blasted out of the speakers, bodies bounced and writhed together—very few of them anything remotely like a virgin.

Joe leaned back against the bar, his sweaty T-shirt clinging to his skin where it pressed against the cold railing. The bass throbbed through his body, vibrating his core. He'd never danced like he had tonight.

He didn't even need Chris at his side, egging him on, and telling him not to worry about what people thought. He'd been right to come down to London. He should listen to his friend more often.

There was work for him here, surely. He didn't need the security, or oppression, of home any more. Chris had promised to help find him something, if he wanted to stay. Right now, he could think of nothing better.

Chris sauntered up and grabbed him by the arm, dragging him back towards the middle of the dance floor.

"I can't," Joe protested half-heartedly. "I need a break. I need a drink."

He didn't need any more to drink at all, he was already stumbling as Chris led him across the heaving floor.

The young French guys he'd been dancing with earlier caught his eye.

The sexy one was called Luc, but Joe couldn't remember the other guy's name. Something with a G. It didn't matter, "Mate" would do. He'd pretty much ignored Joe all night anyway, spending most of it leaning against the bar looking sultry.

Luc, on the other hand, had been flirting with Joe all night. And Joe wasn't really sure how to handle it. No one had ever hit on him before. Sure enough, Luc touched Joe's waist as he passed, and the look he gave him made Joe's stomach do somersaults. Joe let his own hand rest on Luc's for a moment. Holding back long enough for Luc to whisper in his ear.

"Come dance with me."

His breath smelled of beer and cigarettes. His accent was amazing. His lips close enough to kiss. And Joe knew he could, but still he hesitated. Apart from Chris, he'd never kissed anyone. Not like that. And that had only been the one time.

Chris always joked that just one kiss from him had spoiled Joe for other men. He may have been right once, but Joe had moved on. And no one—not even Chris—had ever looked at him the way Luc just had. For the first time in their friendship, Joe suddenly wanted Chris to just disappear.

"I'll be back," Joe called to Luc, as Chris dragged him on through the throng of dancers. Luc smiled as gyrating bodies closed the space between them. A squeal rose above the beat, and Joe turned to see Chris planting a full kiss on the lips of a tall woman in a tight red sequined dress which framed her stunning figure.

"Get off, you bugger! You'll smear my lippy."

Liverpudlian accent. Cheekbones to die for. Nails like knife blades. Red wig piled high, with a little curl teased down each temple. Six foot something in heels, and eye shadow that made Cindy Lauper look like she wasn't even trying.

The sequins glistened in the disco lights, making her look like she was made of glitter.

Up close, Joe could see make-up caking around a tiny missed patch of stubble. Barely noticeable, and it took nothing away from the overall effect. He was dumbstruck. *You're not in Kansas now.*

"Patty, darling," Chris gushed. "You look fabulous."

That was Chris all over, as enthusiastic as a puppy, as practical as a chocolate teapot. He just wanted everyone to be happy and Joe loved him for it, even if he had just disregarded three years of a psychology degree and a decent enough job in social services.

As "Girls Just Wanna Have Fun" took over the speakers, Joe scanned the room, half-looking for Chris, but mostly taking in the strange mix of people: trendies and trannies, artists and arseholes.

Even the handful of self-conscious, floppy-haired New Romantics didn't look too far out of place, lounging on the raised sofas in the corner, scowling their disdain at the surrounding revellers. The club was a proper melting pot, and Joe was loving the easy anonymity of it all.

He looked over at Luc, who had reached the front of the bar queue, leaning in to get the barman's attention. His dark hair was a pile of soft curls with closely shaved sides. His pale brown eyes were almost golden and they danced when he spoke. Luc glanced over, caught Joe staring and winked. Joe's stomach did a flip. He was totally smitten already.

Luc turned his attention back to the bar, just as the barman began serving a tough-looking girl with pink tips to her bleach-blonde hair. Luc looked back at Joe and shrugged. Joe smiled.

"I'm going to the loo," Joe mouthed at him, pointing to the dark corner at the back of the club where the toilets were. Luc nodded.

Joe weaved his way through the crowd, smiling at the strange collection of dancers, not minding that they bumped and jostled him as he passed. Sticky floors and sticky skin. A slice of a strange new heaven.

He caught a glimpse of Chris, standing beside a concrete pillar with his back to the room, and headed over. He was about to pounce on him when he realised that Chris was not alone.

In the dark recess behind the pillar was an older man: heavy-set, broad-shouldered, tough-looking, with a black trilby hat pulled low over his eyes, and the collar of his thick, dark coat up, covering his chin. He must be boiling in here. Joe could tell by his body language that he was not happy with Chris.

Chris looked at the floor, cowed by this stranger. Joe took a few steps closer. The music was too loud to hear what the man was saying. Was Chris in some kind of trouble? Should he help?

He watched the man's fat finger pointing close to Chris's face, his other hand gripping Chris's wrist tightly. A warning, harshly issued. Chris looked as though he was trying to protest, but the man gave him one final word and Chris nodded a subdued, reluctant agreement.

The man bumped Chris's shoulder as he stalked off, parting a way through the crowded floor and pushing through a set of doors marked "private—staff only". Chris didn't move for a moment. His shoulders raised and slumped in a big sigh and he shook his head.

Joe slipped away quickly into the darker corridor leading towards the toilets. He didn't want Chris to know he'd seen the exchange. He'd only be more upset. Chris liked to maintain his reputation as a cool, controlled guy and he hated anyone seeing the cracks.

Joe glanced back and saw Chris coming right towards him. He ducked into the toilets quickly. Perhaps he'd catch Chris in there and make sure he was alright without letting him know he'd seen anything.

Inside, he kept his eye on the mirrors; watching the door as he stood at the urinal, but Chris didn't appear. Joe finished, washed his hands and splashed some cool water on his face, drying himself ineffectually with the bottom of his T-shirt, before pushing back through the door into the corridor.

"I can't believe you're doing this! You're such an arsehole."

Joe stopped in front of the door just as it swung shut. The voice was Patty's. Cracking with emotion. Angry and upset. Joe peered into the gloom at the end of the corridor, far from the bustle of the club, and saw Chris and Patty, face to face, mid-argument.

Chris muttered something urgent and placatory. It didn't work. Patty was trembling with rage.

"You promised, Chris."

"I know," Chris said, his voice tight, tense. "I'm sorry."

Patty raised a hand to slap him but Chris caught it. Patty's shoulders slumped, the personality stripped bare. With the glamour and vitality suddenly gone, Joe saw Patty now as nothing more than a nervous young man in a flamboyant outfit, not sure if he could carry it off.

"You just do whatever you want, all the time, and you don't care who you hurt."

"That's not fair," Chris snapped.

"It's true."

Joe tucked himself in against the wall, close enough to hear, but far enough away to remain discreet.

"You'll be great," Chris said, holding both Patty's hands in his. Even from this distance, Joe could see the tears welling in Patty's eyes.

"Oh, just fuck off, Chris," she snapped. "I could kill you sometimes."

The sound of the dressing room door slamming echoed up the corridor. Chris punched the wall with the side of his fist, swearing at the closed door.

Joe hurried back into the club before Chris could turn around and find him there. Whatever was going on with his friend, he was sure Chris wouldn't want him to know about either of the conversations he'd just witnessed.

CHRIS SHRUGGED OFF his annoyance, took a deep breath and headed back towards the dance floor. He still needed to find Joe and let him know he was leaving the club.

He lifted himself up to a small platform beside the bar to get a better view of the club floor, and finally spotted Joe in a dark corner, wrapped around Luc. He allowed himself a grin. It was good to see his old friend relaxing a bit. He'd missed having him around. Joe was the only link to his old life that Chris still enjoyed, and the only real friend he'd ever had.

He didn't feel too bad about ducking out early on their night out. Joe would be fine with his little Frenchman. Luc was a nice guy. Chris should know, he'd spent most of last week getting to know Luc's friend, Gabriel. And they'd had a lot of fun.

Besides, Chris hoped that a little fling with Luc would mean Joe would stop giving him those puppy-dog eyes. It was very sweet, but he didn't fancy Joe, and he never had. He loved him, but he didn't fancy him. He touched Joe's shoulder, not wanting to interrupt.

"I've got to head out for a bit," Chris whispered into his ear— the one that didn't have a hot Frenchman's tongue in it. "Don't do anything I wouldn't do."

"Where are you going?" Joe asked, frowning. Luc looked up and smiled at Chris before turning his attention back to Joe's neck.

"Something's come up. I need to go. I'll see you back at mine later."

He planted a kiss on Joe's cheek and pressed a door key into his hand.

"Don't wait up," Chris said, turning his back on Joe and Luc and twisting his way through the heaving dance floor before his friend could ask any more questions.

He hadn't lied, specifically. He definitely needed to get out of that club. Chris had learned the hard way that Tony Lagorio wasn't the kind of guy who took no for an answer. The Lizard, as he was known, was ruthless at the best of times, and Chris had just been given a very clear ultimatum. Unfortunately, it wasn't one he was able to deliver on yet. He had stuff to do, and quickly.

As he left the dance floor, Patty walked out onto the stage, beginning a smouldering rendition of "Fever" to cheers and whistles. Chris turned back, put his fingers at the sides of his mouth and issued a piercing wolf-whistle of his own to encourage her.

He knew the song had been chosen with him in mind, and he felt bad leaving now, but if he didn't, Patty would only insist on coming with him later, and he couldn't have that.

Patty—Paul as Chris knew him better—would forgive him, eventually, for walking out during her first ever public drag performance.

Chris burst through the club doors and the cold night air hit him like a wall. His thin jacket might have been stylish, but it was less than useless against the freezing drizzle. His breath fogged in front of him.

More out of habit than desire, he pulled a cigarette from the scrunched up pack in his pocket and cupped his hand around the end, protecting the flame as he lit up. The doors swung closed behind him, shutting out the sound of Patty's warbling.

The street was quiet. It was already late. Pink and red neon lights offering girls, sex and fun reflected off the oily, damp pavement. Chris blew out a thin line of smoke and shivered. He set off towards the all-night café on the corner. A strong coffee would clear his head, and he definitely needed a clear head tonight.

The café had large single-pane windows, looking out over the street. A couple of girls—punks in pink and black—sat at a table by the window, staring at him as he walked in, expressions barely shifting as he smiled at them. He turned his back on them and then blew a quick kiss over his shoulder. *Cheer up, love.* He grinned, but their aggressive snarls remained fixed.

He ordered a coffee to take away, loaded it with a couple of sachets of sugar, and topped it up with milk from an old jug by the till. Chris took another drag of his cigarette and stubbed it out in the ashtray on the counter. He blew on his coffee, took a sip, and headed for the door.

As he hit the road again, a dark car pulled up alongside him. He kept his head down and kept walking. He didn't have time for weirdos trying to pick him up. Not tonight. The car edged forward again, stopping just in front of him. The passenger door swung open. Chris bent down to tell the driver where to go.

"Oh, it's you," he said. "What do you want?"

"Get in. We need to talk."

He did.

·

2.

JOE FLOATED THROUGH the streets on his own little cloud of pure satisfaction. The hour before dawn in Soho was a strange time indeed. A pair of tired-looking prostitutes, still holding out hope for a last, late punter, cat-called to him, offering a good deal. *Not my type, love.*

He reached up to slap a street sign as he turned the corner into the square opposite Chris's flat, chirping a cheerful "alright?" as he dodged a council worker pushing a dustcart along the pavement. He got a sullen "piss off" in reply.

Joe grinned, shrugging. Nothing could shake his mood right now. Not a grumpy bugger in a miserable job. Not the icy morning air. Not even the fact that he'd spent most of his money for the weekend on one night out. *But what a night!*

His T-shirt was still damp under the jacket he'd borrowed from Luc, his sweat long since turned cold. His head buzzed with snatches of remembered conversation and his lips were swollen and tingling, the skin on his chin raw from stubble-burn. He had never kissed, or been kissed, like that before.

He and Luc had hung out together all night, moving on from the club to a little Italian coffee place on Frith Street which seemed to be open all hours—*Bar Italia.* It sounded so exotic and sophisticated, and in its own way, it was. Red and white formica tables, huge, gleaming silver machines spurting out delicious smelling coffee and whistling blasts of steam. A giant black-and-white poster of Rocky Marciano, gloved hands raised, about to unleash his might on a punchball.

The place had a vibrant energy far different to the club, but, like so much of Soho, everyone seemed welcome and the noise levels were high. They had perched in a corner, Joe and Luc, talking, laughing, and flirting as their coffees went cold.

Afterwards, they had gone back to the grotty little hotel Luc was staying in. There was still no sign of Luc's friend, and they had fallen straight into bed, tearing each other's clothes off, mouths locked, hearts pounding. Finally, he'd left Luc sleeping, with a scrawled note on the bedside table giving him Chris's address and an invitation to come find them later. He hoped he would.

Despite the early hour, there were a few people out—late night revellers, early starters, lost wanderers. They all shared the same pavements if not the same mood. A light frost glistened on the paving stones, reflecting the flickering signs from the sex shops which lurked behind every other doorway. Strings of fairy lights—leftover from Christmas—hung from lamp posts and gave the street an oddly innocent, magical feel.

Soho had a particular smell, he'd noticed—damp and slightly stale, coffee brewing, food frying, beer, cigarettes, old buildings breathing. He loved it. It made him feel alive. Such a stark difference to the quiet little town where he and Chris had grown up.

Joe realised it was the first time he'd thought about Chris for hours. He wondered whether he'd be back yet—he'd said he'd be home later, but now dawn was already creeping in. Joe hoped Chris wouldn't be too upset that he'd stayed out all night.

Chris had introduced Joe to the French boys in the first place, and he'd seemed quite happy when Joe had hooked up with Luc, but Chris's moods were notoriously volatile, and he'd grown used to being in control of Joe's feelings and actions. He demanded loyalty, and could sometimes fly into an irrational temper if he thought he was losing it.

Joe stopped at the edge of the square, momentarily unsure of which way to go. All the streets looked the same around here— narrow houses with small doors, set back from the street, with multiple doorbells up the walls of each.

He headed left, following his instincts, and quickly found the blue door beside the narrow alleyway which marked the top of Chris's road.

Turning into the road, he heard footsteps rushing up from behind him. Two skinhead lads, all bovver boots, bomber jackets and bad attitudes, were bearing down on him. He tried to dodge out of their way, but was just a little too slow. One of them shouldered him viciously into the wall.

"Watch it," the skinhead threatened. His friend laughed, and lunged at Joe, eyes wild and menacing, stopping just short of head-butting him as Joe flinched back into the wall.

Spitting at his feet, the skinhead backed off, and they moved on, shouting their goading taunts about poofs into the night air for all to hear. Pocket rebels, looking for a fight.

Joe's heart beat in his throat, and, as he took a deep breath to calm himself, he heard a stifled sob from the narrow alleyway he'd just passed. His stomach sank. What had those lads done?

Cautiously, he moved back to the alleyway. It was dark, with just one flickering lamp providing any light. Another sob in the shadows, and Joe saw a tall, thin woman in high heels, half bent over, leaning against the wall.

"Hey, are you okay? Do you need any help?" Joe asked.

The woman kept her head down, refusing to look up as Joe stepped into the alleyway, her hands covering her face.

"Just fuck off," she said, her voice low and cracking.

A voice Joe thought he recognised. Just like he recognised the tight red sequinned dress, sparkling in the dim light, and the killer heels kicked off on the ground.

"Patty?"

Patty looked up at him, pulling the wig off to reveal a stocking cap. The boy that looked back at him was scared, clutching the bright-red wig in hands streaked with what looked like dirt.

"What happened?" Joe asked, stepping forward. "Are you hurt?"

Without the wig, Joe could see the young man's features more clearly. His mascara had run, and clumps of black stuck to the puffy skin beneath his eyes. His lipstick was smudged across his cheek, and there was something else there. Not dirt, but blood.

Joe rushed forward to help, but got pushed back with surprising force as Patty barged past him and hurried away, barefoot into the night. Joe ran to the end of the alley, looking both ways, but Patty was already gone.

Joe turned back into the alley, collected both shoes from the ground, shocked and confused. Patty, or whatever his real name was, had obviously got into some kind of trouble. Had he come over to carry on the fight he and Chris had started earlier? Joe hoped not, or Chris would be in an unbearable mood, and Joe didn't want anything to ruin his buzz. He hurried towards Chris's flat, the heels dangling from his hand.

Reaching the door, he fished the key out of his pocket, his cold fingers scraping painfully on his tight jeans, but when he went to slip the key into the lock, he realised the door was unlocked. A streak of blood here too, just below the lock. He pushed on the door and, as it swung open, the smell hit him straight away—metallic and meaty.

The high heels fell from his hand and clattered on the doorstep as the reality of the scene in front of him hit home. A body lay on the floor in the hallway, in a pool of blood covering the black-and-white tiles. Legs bent awkwardly, head at an unnatural angle, face battered and bruised. Chris's face. Chris's head. Chris's legs. Joe stumbled into the hallway, his mouth open in a scream that was yet to erupt.

He wasn't aware when his screaming started, or that a door had opened further down the hallway, or that Chris's flatmate, Russell, had come hurtling down the stairs, dressing gown billowing out behind him, or that Chris's blood was seeping into the hem of Russell's gown as he bent beside Chris's body and checked his pulse.

Joe didn't flinch when Russell yelled at the downstairs neighbours to get back in their house and wait for the police. He didn't object when Russell wrapped his arms around him and guided him though his best friend's blood and up the stairs towards the flat.

Everything was happening in a bubble, removed from reality. Sounds, smells, thoughts were all far away and unreal. Their feet on the steps, the urgent voices from the neighbour's flat, the gentle wafting smell of old cigarette smoke from Chris's jacket, which Russell had scooped off the steps as they'd passed and now clutched in his hand, right beside Joe's face. There was a small spot of blood on the collar—nothing compared to the pool on the floor, but it drew Joe's attention like a beacon.

He let Russell guide him up the stairs and into the small kitchen where he slumped, numb and shaking, into one of the chairs at the tiny kitchen table. He heard Russell out in the hallway, calling the police. He heard the words "attacked" and "killed", but they weren't real. None of this was real. *Was it?*

Russell came back into the kitchen, muttering that the police were on their way, but Joe didn't respond. His hands were shaking, tears streaked his face. He finally became aware of the rumble of

17

the kettle boiling and he looked up, half-expecting to see his friend leaning casually against the counter, smoking one of his trademark roll-ups.

But he wasn't there. Russell stood there instead, in his blood-stained gown, his hands pressed firmly on the counter to stop his own shoulders shaking, staring out of the window as the blue flashing lights pulled up outside.

JOE AND RUSSELL HAD been told to stay in the flat and wait while the police did their work downstairs. Neither spoke. Neither knew what to say. They barely even looked at each other. Russell had made them both several cups of sweet tea, which they had consumed in a fog of disbelief, anger and grief.

Joe felt numb. None of it made sense. Chris couldn't be dead. He just couldn't. But Joe knew it was true from the ashen look on Russell's face when he'd come back into the flat, when he'd uttered those fateful words that the police had confirmed—suspected murder. The two of them had collapsed into hard kitchen chairs and stared at each other in disbelief as the tears began to well again. It was true, but it just wouldn't sink in.

After a while sitting in silence, waiting for the police to come up and take their statements, Russell got up decisively, gathering his gown around him.

"I'm going for a shower," he said, and disappeared down the hallway. Joe heard the fan come on in the bathroom, and the sound of water splashing into the bath. He looked at his own hands, holding his fingers up to examine the smudges of Chris's blood. How had that got there? Had he touched Chris's body? Tried to help him? He couldn't remember.

He pushed the chair back and crossed to the sink, running the water over his hands and rubbing distractedly, continuously until there was no sign of blood any more. Washed away. Just like that.

Drying his hands on his jeans, Joe stared out of the window, watching the scene unfolding on the street below. A small crowd loitered in the square, craning their necks to see what all the fuss was about.

A single, uniformed officer stood on the road in front of their door, shepherding any passers-by off the pavement and out of the way. The official, dispassionate comings and goings that accompanied the discovery of a dead body on a London street.

He watched as the crowd of onlookers lost interest after Chris's body, safely wrapped in the black body bag, was loaded into the back of the wagon, already turning away to shrug at each other as the doors slammed.

He was rocked by a sudden urge to sprint down the stairs and stop them from taking his friend away, to hold him one last time. *How had this happened?*

The uniformed policeman stepped aside, disappearing from sight, and Joe shuddered as the first members of the public walked past the spot where his friend had laid, craning to see a glimpse of the horror through the open door. *What was wrong with people?* He wanted to shout at them to go away, to leave them alone.

But he didn't shout. He didn't do anything. All he could do was stare forlornly out of the window, slowly realising that he would never see Chris again. Russell came up and stood beside him, arm around his shoulder, and slowly turned him away from the window.

When Joe looked up at him, he realised that he, too, had been crying. Joe let his head rest on Russell's shoulder, feeling the weight of the awful truth they all now shared. Chris was gone.

A man knocked sharply on the open flat door. Russell looked up and pushed Joe away quickly. Too quickly.

The man—clearly police—hesitated at the door, saying nothing. His long, beige trench coat hung loosely around narrow shoulders. His ratty face pinched in distaste, his eyes darting between Russell and Joe, the judgement barely concealed.

"Come in if you have to," Russell said, bitterly, swiping the two empty tea cups from the table and putting them in the sink.

The man stepped in, his tongue flicking across thin lips as he cast his gaze around the kitchen. He kept his hands held tight in front of him as though scared of anything touching him, and yet there was an arrogance in his eyes—a gleam that made Joe feel he was enjoying this moment too much. The man cleared his throat, locking eyes with Russell.

"Mr Dixon," he said, emphasising the Mr. "I need to ask you a few questions about your... friend." The pause was loaded with inference, the word friend a sneering insinuation. "We can do it here, if you're more comfortable. I shouldn't think you'd want to come down to the station."

His smile was insincere. Joe hated him already.

"Take a seat, Detective Skinner," Russell said, pulling a chair back from the table and sitting down himself. Joe did the same, lining himself up between Russell and the visitor, feeling instinctively protective. *Detective Skinner*. Russell had been a detective too, Chris had told him. There was obviously history between Russell and this weasel-faced man.

"I'd rather stand," Skinner said.

"Suit yourself."

"What can you tell me about Christopher Sexton then? You two were obviously... close." No hint of sympathy.

"He was my tenant."

Skinner snorted.

"Paid you rent, did he? I'll bet."

TAINTED LOVE

The emphasis on the word rent was an obvious jibe and Russell rose to it immediately, lurching across the table and grabbing Skinner by the throat, squeezing until his face started to redden. Joe stood up and pulled him away.

"Don't, Russell. He's not worth it."

Skinner straightened himself up, shrugging his shoulders to readjust his shirt. He was trying to look unfazed, but Joe could see he'd been surprised by the ferocity of Russell's reaction. There was clearly no love lost here.

Russell turned to the sink, rinsing the cups as a distraction, trying to compose himself.

"What do you want to know, Detective?" Joe asked, sounding far more level-headed than he felt.

"And you are?"

"Joseph Stone. Joe. I've known Chris since we were four."

Skinner assessed him disdainfully. Joe refused to flinch under the scrutiny. He hadn't even changed his T-shirt from last night, his hair was a mess, his eyes probably puffy and red. He didn't care. *Judge all you like, you don't know me.*

"When did you last see the victim?" Skinner asked eventually, turning back to Russell.

The victim.

"At around eleven, eleven-thirty," Joe said.

"Well, which is it? Eleven or eleven-thirty?" Skinner sniffed.

"Closer to eleven-thirty, I suppose," Joe replied. "There was an act on. He left the club just as the performance started."

"The club?"

"Gossip's," Joe replied. "We'd been there most of the night. It was a friend's party."

Skinner raised an eyebrow.

"And Chris just left halfway through? Did he say where he was going?"

21

"No, he just said something had come up and he had to go. Said he'd see me back here later."

"Did he seem anxious? Nervous? Upset?"

"No…"

That wasn't true. Joe looked at Russell, who was leaning against the sink, staring at his hands, fingers fidgeting with one another. Russell glanced at him, the slightest frown on his brow. Had he noticed the slight hesitation in Joe's voice?

Joe hadn't had chance to get over the shock of finding Chris yet, let alone tell Russell what he'd seen in the club—the big man in the trilby hat, with hands like spades, telling Chris off. Or the fight Chris had with Patty. Or that Patty, or whoever he was really, had been in the alleyway, with blood on his hands and face. *Had Patty done this?*

Joe tensed, realising that he knew a lot more than he was saying. Something told him he should discuss it with Russell before he told Detective Skinner anything. He had a bad feeling about this policeman.

"And you can't think of anyone he may have fallen out with?" Skinner continued. "Anyone who would want to hurt him?"

"Hurt him?" Joe spluttered. "They didn't just hurt him, they bloody killed him!"

Russell caught Joe's eye and gave a barely perceptible shake of the head, the tiniest warning to keep his cool. Skinner clocked the glance between them and his eyes narrowed.

"He was a popular kid," Russell said quickly. "He had a lot of friends. I can't imagine anyone wanting to do… that. Not to him."

Skinner raised an eyebrow again, looking hard at both of them in turn before sighing.

"So, he left the club alone," Skinner summarised. "And you came home to find him in the hallway. What time was that?"

"I don't know," Joe stammered, reliving the moment he'd come through the door only too vividly.

"We called you straight away," Russell said, protectively. "Just before seven this morning."

"And where were you all night then, between eleven-thirty when you last saw him and seven this morning?"

Joe looked down, glanced at Russell, sighed.

"I met a guy, we went on for coffee when the club closed, and then we went back to his hotel."

"Did he have a name, this guy? Or was discretion part of the transaction?" Skinner didn't even try to hide his disgust.

"Luc," Joe muttered.

"Luke what?"

"I don't know. He's French."

What does it matter where he's from? Joe realised he was babbling. *Why should I feel embarrassed?* He raised his eyes to glare at Skinner.

"And he'll vouch for your movements, will he? This Frenchman?"

"Of course," Joe snapped. "Why wouldn't he?"

"You never know with you lot," Skinner muttered, almost inaudibly.

He sniffed again and turned to Russell.

"And you, Mr Dixon?" he asked, a sardonic note to his voice. "Where were *you* while all this was going on?"

"I was here all night," Russell said.

"You were upstairs all the time the attack was happening, were you?"

Russell looked up slowly, his eyes filled with hate.

"It would appear so," he said, flatly.

"And you didn't hear anything?"

"No."

"Because it was quite a brutal attack," Skinner seemed to be enjoying twisting the knife. "So I would imagine there would have been a fair bit of noise. You didn't hear anything at all?"

"I was asleep."

Russell sounded defensive. Joe frowned. Had Russell heard the attack and stayed upstairs, not wanting to get involved? Surely not. He was a former policeman, he wouldn't sit quietly by while someone was being attacked. Skinner folded his arms across his chest, recognising a stonewall when he saw one.

"I'll tell you what I know about your young tenant then, shall I?" he asked, leaning back in his chair. "Because I've met him a few times over the years. We've arrested him for being drunk and disorderly. We've arrested him for soliciting. We've had to caution him for assaulting a police officer during a protest. He's a known drug user. And we know only too well the kind of company he keeps. So, I'm afraid it's come as no surprise he's ended up how he has."

He stared at Russell coldly, willing him to challenge him again. Russell's jaw clenched, but he didn't move and said nothing. Silence hung in the room.

"Look," Skinner said, standing up and straightening his coat, "we've got nothing to go on here. As far as we're concerned, he hooked up with someone, brought them back here, things turned ugly, and he came out the worst for it. We've got no witnesses, you claim there's no motive, and I've got no reason to waste valuable police time on yet another dead rent boy. So, if either of you think of something else, let me know. Otherwise, I'm done here."

"He's a good kid," Russell protested.

"Was," corrected Skinner. "But I doubt that. I'll be in touch."

He walked out, leaving the door to the hallway ajar. His footsteps light and carefree on the stairs, the sound of whistling following him out.

TAINTED LOVE

Neither of them moved until the front door slammed and Russell picked up a glass from the draining rack and threw it at the wall, the crystal shards exploding into the hallway. Joe flinched. Silence flooded back into the room.

"He's not going to do anything, is he?" Joe said, eventually.

"No," Russell said, shaking his head.

Shards of broken glass crunched beneath his feet as he pulled a broom out of the hall cupboard and began sweeping. His hands were shaking.

"But don't they have to take it seriously?" Joe asked quietly. "It's murder."

"They should. But they won't. Believe me," Russell said, sweeping the glass into a dustpan. "As far as they're concerned, he's just another stupid little queer who fell foul on a bad hook up. They'll be glad to get him off the streets. And they're certainly not going to dedicate any resources to finding out what happened. Especially not Detective Skinner."

"You know him?" Joe asked, looking up at Russell.

Russell shrugged angrily, throwing the broken glass into the bin and slamming the lid.

"Yes," he said, finally. "I used to work with him. In fact, I used to be his boss. Which is exactly how I know he'll do nothing."

"Can't we file a complaint about him or something?" Joe asked.

"Oh grow up," Russell snapped. "They don't care about people like us. You heard him. He's already written Chris off as a rent boy who picked the wrong guy to bring home. The police don't care. Half the time, they're the ones attacking us."

Joe slumped, feeling suddenly childish. He had just assumed the police would want to prioritise catching Chris's killer. But why should they? They must see hundreds of crimes like this every year. There were always stories about gay-bashings, or random beatings, or unsolved murders. Chris would be just another statistic, not worth the manpower.

"I should have said something," Joe blurted.

"About what?"

"About last night. I saw Chris talking to someone in the club," Joe said.

Russell rolled his eyes.

"That doesn't mean anything," he sniffed.

"No, I mean, not just some guy. Not like that. He didn't look like he belonged there, you know? He was big. Huge hands. And he looked really angry, like he was telling Chris off."

Russell sat down opposite him and poured them both a hefty shot of brandy.

"What did he look like?" Russell asked.

"Big. Trilby hat. Heavy wool coat. And it was boiling in there."

"Oh shit," Russell said, downing his brandy and topping up the glass.

"You know who it was?"

"Tony Lagorio," Russell said, as though the name itself could conjure the devil. "People call him the Lizard."

"The Lizard?"

"You don't want to know," Russell replied. "Suffice to say, he's a nasty piece of work, and you don't want to end up on his bad side."

"You think he killed Chris?"

"No," Russell said. "When he hurts anyone, he makes damn sure people know it was him that did it. He likes his messages to be clear."

"How does he not get arrested?"

Russell smiled at his naivety.

"Believe me, I tried. I think you need to lower your opinion of the police a few notches, kid," he said. "Tony's a gangster, through and through. He's got most of the force in his pocket. Any time he needs a favour from the boys in blue, all he has to do is ask. I tried to bring him in a couple of times. Something always happened to the evidence, or to the bust itself. I probably know more about him now than his own mother does, and none of it would make her proud. Problem was, I could never make any of it stick."

"How did Chris know him?"

"Chris owed him money at one point," Russell replied. "But he told me he'd paid it off."

"Why would Chris owe someone like him money?" Joe asked.

"Tony stumped up Chris's half of the money to set up the fashion label," Russell said. "I told him it was a stupid idea, taking money from the Lizard, but Chris always knows best."

He paused, catching himself still using the present tense. It would take a while.

"I would have paid it off for him if I could," Russell continued. "But I couldn't afford it. And he wouldn't let me, anyway."

Joe frowned. The idea was preposterous—Chris's family were rich and, though they didn't approve of his lifestyle, Joe was sure they'd never let their boy go without. Would they?

At school, Chris had always been the kid with the best trainers, the nicest lunches, the newest toys. If he'd needed money, he could have just gone back to his dad and asked. Or had things really got that bad between them that Chris would rather get into debt with a gangster than see his father?

What the hell had Chris got himself into? Joe had thought that his friend had seemed far more relaxed and in control of his life than he'd ever seen before. With his nice flat, a good circle of friends, his fashion label growing stronger by the day—he'd seemed genuinely settled. Had that all just been a show?

"I also saw him arguing with Patty," Joe said. "His drag queen friend."

27

"He was arguing with Paul?"

"If that's his name," Joe shrugged. "They were in the corridor. Patty told him to fuck off."

"Well, if Chris was going to leave the club before Patty's show even started, Paul had every right to be pissed off. The whole performance was for Chris, after all. Poor old Paul is besotted with him."

Joe took a nerve-steadying sip of his own brandy. It burned, but it felt necessary.

"Just before I came back and found Chris, I saw him again. In the alley, at the end of the road. In a right state. I recognised the dress."

Russell scrutinised him—topped up both glasses.

"He had blood on his face," Joe blurted. "I thought he'd been attacked, but maybe he came back here to finish the argument with Chris, and it turned into a fight. Maybe he killed Chris. I should have told that detective what I saw."

Russell reached a hand out to hold Joe's.

"You need to calm down," he said. "I know this is a lot to take in, but they were friends. Paul would never hurt Chris. Not like that. He loved him more than anyone."

Joe could feel the anger boiling inside him. Chris was *his* friend. *He* loved him. More than Paul or Russell or any of his new friends ever could. And Paul had been right here, skulking in the alleyway with Chris's blood on his hands, and tears streaking his face. Either he killed him, or he knew something about what had happened last night. Joe stood up purposefully.

"Where are you going?" Russell asked.

"I'm going to find that detective and tell him what I saw."

Russell shot to his feet, blocking Joe's exit.

"Sit down," he said.

They stood face to face, neither backing off.

TAINTED LOVE

"Look," Russell said. "I know you're upset. Of course you are, you loved him and what's happened is terrible. But I can promise you that going back to that so-called detective with any of what you've just told me will end up with Paul being arrested and them throwing away the key. No questions asked."

"Good," Joe spat, but he already knew it would be wrong. He sat down heavily.

"The police aren't interested in the truth," Russell said. "Well, not that lot anyway. Not when it comes to our sort. If you give them a reason to arrest Paul, they'll take it and make the rest of the evidence fit. It won't help Paul, it won't help you, and it sure as hell won't help find who really did this to Chris."

"But we have to do something," Joe said.

"I know," Russell said. "And we will."

RUSSELL SAT ALONE at the kitchen table, his head reeling and his hands trembling gently. His old police instincts had kicked in the moment he'd heard the scream from downstairs and discovered poor Joe standing over his best friend's body. The kid would take a while to get over that.

Russell had slipped into autopilot as he'd cleared the scene, called the police, escorted Joe upstairs for sweet tea and brandy, and waited for the detectives to turn up and take statements.

Now that Skinner had gone, and Joe was in the shower cleaning himself up, Russell had a moment to think for the first time.

He had seen more than his fair share of corpses in his time on the force, and he'd watched enough of his friends die in recent years, but this was different. Chris had been such a dynamic force, a whirlwind of lively enthusiasm, constantly getting into scrapes, relentlessly moving, always on the go. Not any more. Just like that—a brilliant life snuffed out and all that potential, all that energy, just vanished into thin air.

He looked at Chris's jacket hanging over the back of the chair, one of Chris's new designs, the bright yellow collar now stained with his blood.

He'd gathered up Chris's wallet from the ground outside the flat, noticing straight away that it was empty of cash. Unusual for Chris on a big night out. He'd had money worries before, but recently Chris had been doing well, and was never short of a few bob. Perhaps there was something to Skinner's mugging theory after all.

He had also found Chris's small instamatic camera on the floor. Slim, silver and black, Chris always joked that it was his spy camera. Said it made him feel like James Bond. And he carried it everywhere, snapping inspirations for his shows, or quick camera tests for cute guys he promised could be his models.

And yet, when Russell had found it, the back was open and there was no film inside. If Chris had been mugged, surely the camera would have gone the same way as the money. So, whoever had killed Chris had taken the film and left the camera. But why?

Russell knew he should have mentioned it to Skinner, but his former colleague would have just buried both items in an evidence box and left them to gather dust. He'd already made his mind up about this case and had made it clear he wasn't planning on conducting much of an investigation. If there were clues to be found, Russell would have to find them himself.

He sat back in the chair, feeling the flimsy Formica seat back creak beneath his bulk. He'd let himself go since leaving the force. He needed to get back in shape.

He smiled sadly. Chris was always nagging him to get fitter, get back out there and start dating properly. He kept promising he would, knowing that he'd need some kind of catalyst to pull himself out of the depressive cloud that had threatened to swallow him up when he was forced from the job. And here it was.

Was he really going to do this? Was he actually going to investigate Chris's murder on his own? If he'd still been on the force, he would have been removed from the case for being too close to the victim.

But he wasn't on the force any more, was he? Skinner had made sure of that. And he was absolutely sure that Skinner would do nothing about Chris's murder. So unless Russell did something himself, his young flatmate—his friend—would never get justice.

JOE HAD PERSUADED Russell to let him come along to talk to Paul, and was grateful he'd agreed. He'd felt better for a shower and a change of clothes, but he needed to be out of the flat and doing something or he would go mad.

The previous day had been spent in a fog of shock and sadness, drowned in brandy and revived by intermittent moments of anger and odd, uncomfortable levity.

Joe had talked fondly about memories of Chris from their school days. About his ridiculous teenage crush on his best friend. About the fact that Chris had always been so confident of who he was, and how his life would go. The memories had prompted both tears and laughter, each shrouded with the disbelief that Chris was no longer with them.

Russell for his part had shared stories of Chris's time in London, his celebrity friends, his wild parties. It was clear that Chris had been a tonic to Russell. He was so free. So open, while Russell admitted that he'd always struggled to admit his sexuality, not just because of the job. He felt like he'd been brought up in a different time. Chris had opened the door for him to admit who he was. Especially after Russell had been suspended from the force.

At some point in the afternoon, Joe had called his mother. His older sister, Deborah, came to the phone instead, her voice tinged with her usual judgement.

Apparently the police had already informed Chris's parents. Deborah said they were all shocked to hear about the life Chris had been leading. Joe could only imagine what Detective Skinner had told Chris's parents on the phone—their errant son, already known to the police for various petty crimes, had been murdered by some strange man he'd taken home for sex.

Deborah had told Joe to come home immediately. He'd refused. It was the first time in his life he'd properly stood up to her.

He'd never officially come out to his family, but Deborah had guessed years ago. Her disapproval was evident in all the little tuts and glances—the way she watched him, hawk-eyed, with her children. The way she quizzed him about any man he mentioned, from his boss to the kid in the corner shop. The way she tutted, from time to time, especially when he laughed. "So bloody camp," she'd muttered once. She didn't think he'd heard.

To let him know she knew and didn't approve, she'd taken to sending him articles in the post, studiously cut from the papers, espousing the dangers of the rising AIDS epidemic. *The Gay Plague*, according to the tabloids. A new omnipotent killer. Joe never mentioned the articles on the rare occasions they saw each other, and neither did she.

"Mum's very upset," Deborah had said.

"So am I," Joe had replied. He was sick of having to hide from his family, and he wasn't going to let Chris's memory be tarnished by their bigotry.

Russell had helped him handle the aftermath of the call, and by the end of the day, emboldened by booze, they'd agreed to do everything they could to find out what had happened to Chris. And so here they were, hitting the streets together, with no idea where to start.

The late-morning air was crisp and refreshing. The shock of Chris's death still chewed constantly at Joe's stomach, and he knew

33

at some point it would overwhelm him again, but right now he was happy to keep moving. He wanted answers and he was sure Paul had a few of them.

Chris would have laughed at the thought of Joe and Russell as the caped crusaders, stepping in to defend his memory. For now, it was too painful to think of Chris laughing. It was too painful to think of Chris at all. Joe needed to be busy, and this was the perfect way to do that.

Soho was still alive and vibrant, getting on with the day as though nothing had happened. The air was filled with hollering market traders, angry car horns, music from windows above the shops and bars, leering calls from door girls tempting punters into the clubs that had seemed so exotic last night but seemed a little sad at lunchtime.

The streets felt different in the light of day—shabbier, seedier, less glamorous. Or perhaps it was the realisation that everything was different now and would never be the same again.

Russell strode purposefully along the busy pavement, weaving in and out of pedestrians, workers and tourists, managing to bend himself around them without ever touching—a practised Londoner. Joe struggled to keep up.

They finally stopped outside a corner pub called The Red Lion and Russell peered through the window.

"Come on," he said, opening the door and striding in.

The pub smelled of stale cigarettes, spilled beer, sweat and toilets. A couple of career drinkers at the bar looked up as they walked in, but turned quickly back to their pints. The barman stood up from his stool behind the bar as he saw Russell.

"Bit early for you, isn't it?" he asked, smiling.

"Hi Ron," Russell said. "Is Paul in?"

"He's upstairs," Ron confirmed. "He was in a right state when he got back. What's he gone and done now?"

"That's what I'm trying to find out," Russell said. "Mind if we go up?"

"Help yourself," Ron said, raising the bar flap so that they could step through. "Shouldn't think you'll get much out of him though."

Joe felt the barman watching him as he squeezed past. He was a big guy—tall, broad-shouldered, friendly face. Joe smiled, and quickly followed Russell up the narrow flight of stairs.

It was like walking into a different world. The décor here was fresher than downstairs—bright, primary colours covered the walls in bold blocks. The short corridor opened out into a large lounge room, full of modern, predominantly black furniture and clean lines. No sign of the seventies décor from downstairs, this room had embraced everything the eighties had to offer. It felt unnaturally cheerful.

"Paul?" Russell called.

No reply. Russell headed towards the first of three doors off the corridor, poked his head round and quickly turned away, heading to the next.

Joe peered through the half-open door to see the tidy bedroom behind it, all blacks, reds and whites—very modern. Very male. Very straight. Unlikely to be Paul's room.

Russell knocked gently on the next door.

"Paul?" he called again.

"Go away," came the reply. His voice sounded thick.

"Paul, love, we're all upset, but we really need to talk to you," Russell said.

"Leave me alone."

Russell turned the handle, and the door opened a crack. The look he gave Joe told him to stay where he was. Joe heard water splashing as Russell entered the room.

"Jesus. You can't just barge in," Paul shouted.

"I just did, petal. Here, cover yourself up," Russell replied. "We need to talk."

Through the open door, Joe caught a glimpse of Paul wrapping a towel around his waist. His face was clean of any make-up, his hair wet and tousled. He looked completely different out of drag. Smaller, skinnier, and much paler.

Russell put his arm around Paul's shoulder and led him out of the bathroom into the bedroom. He turned back to Joe.

"Kitchen's through there," he pointed. "Get the kettle on and see if you can rustle up some biscuits or something. Anything sweet."

By the time Joe brought three steaming mugs of tea and a half-empty packet of custard cremes back into the lounge, Russell and Paul were already sitting on the bright green sofa, deep in quiet conversation.

Russell held Paul's hands in his own. Paul looked up at Joe with red-rimmed eyes. Joe wanted to feel sorry for him, but he couldn't. Not yet. His own pain was still too raw, and he didn't trust him, even if Russell did.

"So," Joe said, putting all three mugs on the glass coffee table and sitting in an armchair facing the two of them. "Where have we got to? What happened to Chris?"

Paul stammered, unsure where to start. Joe couldn't help but chip in.

"I know you know something," Joe said, testily. "I saw you and Chris arguing in the club, just before he left. What was that about?"

Paul flinched, turning back to Russell, looking for support. Russell squeezed his hand.

"Take it easy, Joe," Russell warned, "we're all friends here."

Joe wasn't so sure about that. He wanted answers.

"I told him to fuck off," Paul blurted. "That was the last thing I said to him."

TAINTED LOVE

Russell glared at Joe as Paul dissolved into wracking sobs again.

"I'm sure you didn't mean it," Russell said gently.

"I did. I was so pissed off with him."

"Why?" Joe asked. "What were you fighting about?"

"He promised to stay and support me, and then just as I was about to go on, he said he had to leave. I couldn't believe he would do that to me. I was doing the whole bloody thing for him, and he wasn't even going to see it."

"Where was he going?" Russell asked.

"He wouldn't say," Paul said. "He just said it was important, and that it couldn't wait. He couldn't even look me in the eye. I was so angry with him."

Paul broke down again. Russell handed him one of the mugs of tea and rubbed his back, giving him time to gather himself again. He gave Joe another stern look, warning him to play nicely. Russell had only agreed to let Joe tag along if he sat quietly and let him do the talking. Joe hadn't managed that very well so far.

Paul sniffed, wiping his eyes with the back of his hand.

"Paul, love," Russell said gently. "I know it's hard. It is for all of us. But you have to be honest with me now. Was Chris in some kind of trouble?"

"What do you mean? What trouble?"

"Joe says he saw Chris talking to Tony Lagorio," Russell said.

"The Lizard?" Paul said, surprised. "Where?"

"In the club," Joe said. "I was heading to the toilets when I saw Chris. He was talking to this big guy and it looked like he was getting a right telling off. I went into the toilets, and when I came out, I saw the two of you arguing and I didn't want to interrupt because it looked quite heated. Then Chris found me at the bar, told me he had to go because something had come up, and that was the last I saw him."

Joe had intended the insinuation about Paul's argument to knock him, but the news about Tony seemed to unsettle him more.

"Tony was in the club?" Paul said, frowning. He looked from Joe to Russell in confusion.

"It's his club, isn't it?" Russell asked. "Why wouldn't he be there? I mean, he *is* one of the owners, right?"

"Yeah, but he never comes into the club. Not when it's open, anyway. He only ever comes when we're clearing up at the end of the night to make sure there's no cash left on the premises. I don't think I've ever seen him in there during opening hours, and I certainly didn't see him there the other night. Mind you, I wasn't working the bar that night, on account of my performance."

"Well, maybe it wasn't him," said Joe. "I mean, I don't know the man. I just saw Chris talking to a big guy in a trilby hat and a heavy, long coat."

"That's Tony," Russell and Paul said together.

"What was so important that Tony had to come down on a Friday night to see Chris? Did he still owe him?" Russell asked.

"No," Paul said. "Chris paid him back ages ago. He was fine financially."

Joe frowned. That didn't sound like the friend he knew. Chris had never been "fine" as far as money was concerned. His family were rich enough, but when he'd refused to join the family accountancy firm they'd as good as cut him off, probably in the hope it would force him to return when his fashion business failed.

Chris hadn't failed, but he *was* hopeless with money—spent it as soon as he got it, and not always on the most important things.

Joe had helped him out several times in the past, when he needed just enough to make his rent payments after he'd ploughed all his money into the business; or a couple of hundred quid to help with living expenses when he'd spent his last tenner on a present for a friend. He would always pay it back, eventually, but Joe had never got the impression that Chris was *fine financially*.

"I know," Russell agreed, "he's had no trouble with rent for the last few months and he's even bought some new things for the flat. He just said the business was doing well."

"Tell that to Gavin," Paul huffed.

Joe saw Russell's head tilt, a narrowing of the eyes. A small penny had just dropped for him. He made a mental note to ask him about it later.

"So," Russell said, "if it wasn't about money, why would Tony have come to find him last night?"

"I don't know," Paul said, desperately. "Honestly, if he was in any kind of trouble with Tony again, we'd have known about it, wouldn't we?"

Russell shrugged, frustrated. A dead end, for now.

"Why did you run away from me last night?" Joe asked, changing tack. "In the alleyway."

Paul got up quickly as though that flight instinct was kicking in again. He crossed to the window and looked out at the street below. So much for keeping quiet and letting Russell do the talking, but there was something going on with Paul, and Joe didn't like it. He hadn't studied psychology for three years to not recognise a guilty complex when he saw one—Paul was holding something back.

"I didn't know what to do," he said quietly, his back to them both. "I'd gone over to see Chris, to make him apologise for leaving me on my own up on the stage. The door was open, so I went in. He was just lying there..."

He turned back to face them, looking pale.

"He was already cold," he said, shuddering. "I tried to make him sit up. I thought there must be something I could do to help him, but he was gone. I panicked. I ran. I'm not proud of it."

"Why didn't you call up to me?"

Paul just shook his head.

"I couldn't..."

"So why were you hiding in the alley?" Joe cut across him.

"I didn't know what to do, I couldn't think. I wanted to get as far away as I could, but I couldn't leave him like that."

"So you hid in the alley?"

"There were these skinheads. They looked like trouble. I thought maybe they'd done it. I thought they'd come for me too if they saw me. I'd come straight from the club, I was still in drag."

"Yeah, I saw them too," Joe said. "Only, they didn't have Chris's blood on them, and you did."

Paul turned on him, lunging forward.

"Are you accusing me of killing Chris?"

Russell stood up between them.

"No one's accusing anyone," he said. "Sit down, both of you."

They both did. He might be short, and a little round in the middle, but when Russell told you to do something, he had an air of authority about him that made you do it without question.

"Why did you run away when I spoke to you?" Joe asked.

"Because I didn't want to talk to you, alright?" Paul said. "Because I didn't want to have to tell you that Chris was dead. I didn't want to say those words out loud because then it would be true."

They sat in silence for a moment, the sounds of the bar below travelling up through the floorboards. The unmistakable strains of "Love is a Stranger" on the jukebox. The clink of glasses. Mumbled chatter. A burst of raucous laughter. The lunchtime crowd was gathering.

"I know I should have done something," Paul said eventually. "I should've called the police, but I didn't know what to say. I should have called you, Russell, but I just couldn't speak. There was so much blood. I'm sorry. Who could do something like that to him?"

It was a question none of them could answer. For now. But at least Joe no longer thought Paul had murdered Chris.

4.

THE FLAT WAS SO QUIET. No noise from the street below. Monday in Soho was an altogether quieter affair, as though the streets and buildings needed time to recover from the weekend. Joe knew he did.

Russell had gone off on his own to try to speak to this Tony Lagorio character. When Joe had asked if that was a good idea, Russell assured him that he would be fine. He was going to Tony's restaurant, and was confident that there was enough of a lunchtime crowd around for him to feel relatively safe. Joe hoped he was right.

Tony had been one of the last people seen speaking to Chris, though, and whatever he'd said had made Chris change his plans quite suddenly. The next thing they knew, Chris was dead.

Given what Russell had told him about Tony Lagorio's history, Joe was glad he didn't have to meet him. He hoped Russell would be alright.

Despite his gruff exterior, Joe could see that Russell had a big heart. He'd obviously enjoyed having Chris share the flat, and he was clearly feeling the loss deeply too. Joe liked him and trusted his instincts. He must have been a good cop in his day.

Joe sat on the end of Chris's bed, feet tucked up under his knees, with echoes of their last moments in that room running through his mind. They'd been getting ready to go out to the club, laughing, messing around—Chris dancing around in front of the mirror, shirtless, lithe, alive. How could he be dead?

He looked at Chris's open wardrobe. Hanging on the inside of each door were two suits from Chris's newest fashion line, one of which Joe had tried on yesterday. He'd let Chris snap some photos of him in that suit, among the others of them both fooling around, full of laughter and enthusiasm for the night ahead.

They were photographs he would never see—Russell had already told him about finding Chris's camera in the hallway, the film removed. Neither Joe nor Russell believed that Chris's death was a mugging gone bad. Somebody had wanted him dead, and that somebody had wanted whatever was on that camera.

What were you involved in, Chris?

Joe crossed to the wardrobes and stroked the soft, bright suit, holding the stitching between his fingers. Stitches that Chris had put there.

Joe ran his fingers over the label inside the suit jacket. The words SEXTON & JONES were picked out in gold thread, with a small crown embroidered over the letter "O" in each name.

What would happen to the company now? According to Chris, he had been the creative talent behind the duo, and his business partner, Gavin, dealt with the money. Would Gavin carry on without him? Had anyone even told him that Chris was dead yet?

Chris had confided in Joe that he and Gavin had been arguing about the new line, and about moving the studio. Chris was determined that they would stay in their original home, but Gavin wanted to move and expand.

Chris had said that Gavin was trying to push him out of the company, but he was resisting the split. "Over my dead body," he'd joked to Joe. There wouldn't be much of a company left anyway, without its star designer.

A fresh wave of sadness forced Joe across the room to the messy little desk in the corner. There was stuff everywhere. Little reminders of the life that had filled this room until so recently. Trinkets, treasures and mementos, suddenly reduced to little more than clutter to be swept away. Chris had been such a dynamic, focussed guy with a bright future ahead of him. How could this have happened?

Sitting at the desk, Joe opened the top drawer. Chris had never been particularly private or possessive of his things, never had any secrets from Joe. Or so he'd thought.

He hesitated before delving into the drawer. What would he find in here? Was he ready to unpack Chris's life like this? He had to if he was going to get to the truth of what had happened.

He removed a neatly stacked pile of photographs of young men wearing a range of Chris's outfits. He didn't recognise any of the models, but they all had that familiar look that Chris favoured: high cheekbones, angular chins, big hair, blue eyes. The opposite of Joe with his short, dark hair and brown eyes.

Beneath the photographs were a couple of dog-eared leaflets from a protest late last year about the threatened closure of the Campbell Centre, a charity-run clinic for people with HIV and AIDS.

Joe remembered Chris trying to get him to join them on that march, but he hadn't been able to get away from work, and if he was honest, he hadn't wanted to get in any trouble. He should have done it. Chris been so passionate about the charity, it would have meant the world to him if Joe had come. Too late for regrets now.

A copy of the front page of the newspaper from the day of the protest showed an image of Chris, front and centre in the line of protesters, hand reaching forward with middle finger raised, mouth open, shouting abuse at the police trying to protect some flustered looking MP. Joe smiled at the image. The world would be a lot smaller without Chris in it.

He absently opened drawer after drawer, pulling out the residual evidence of his friend's life. What would happen to all this stuff? Would Chris's parents want any of it? Would they come and pick over the remains of the young life they'd turned their backs on, tutting their disapproval as they discovered his darker secrets. Would they take any of the blame for how his life had ended, having cast him out instead of supporting him? Joe doubted it.

In the bottom of one drawer, he found a small diary, black and scuffed. "1984" embossed in gold on the front cover.

Flicking it open, he saw Chris's artistic scrawl on the first page: a list of initials with phone numbers beside them. A star system, scribbled beside their numbers, seemed to rate each between one and five stars.

Leafing through the pages, Joe noticed that at least one set of initials had been entered almost every week since September, sometimes two or three sets of initials per week, but never two on the same day.

Passing back and forth between the months, he discovered that some initials recurred regularly. Every other Tuesday afternoon: ECS. The first Friday of each month: LL.

On at least four occasions, there was simply the letter X written large. According to the ratings, X was a five star. Joe found a final reference in early December, where the X had been crossed out, and MJ scribbled in heavily and underlined, followed by an exclamation mark in brackets. The exclamation mark was surprising. Who or what was MJ? Joe wished he could ask Chris what this little code was all about.

He laid the diary on the desk. He would show Russell later. Perhaps there was a simple explanation, but the way the book had been tucked in beneath the clothes at the bottom of the drawer and the secrecy of the initials made him suspicious.

A cork pin board above the desk was filled with all the photographs Chris *had* wanted the world to see. Him and his celebrity friends in clubs, in restaurants, in bars. Actors, musicians, socialites. So-called friends that had welcomed this dynamic and talented young designer into their social circle and made him feel special.

One image, partly concealed by newer ones, showed Chris, shirtless, lying with his head on a man's chest. The man's face was cut out of shot. Chris, as ever, the centre of his own universe. He looked content.

Joe felt angry, jealous tears pricking his eyes and grabbed at the images, tearing them off the board and throwing them in tatters on the floor. They didn't deserve to be part of his memories. They weren't Chris's real friends. Not like Joe was.

As the photographs fluttered to the ground, the realisation hit Joe suddenly, knocking the wind out of him—he hadn't known the real Chris any more than any of those celebrity friends had. And he'd let him down just as badly.

He slumped on the end of the bed, picking up Chris's jacket that Russell had neatly laid out on the covers. More than anything, he wanted to talk to Chris, and he knew he never would again.

He gathered the jacket tight, and curled up on the bed with it clutched to his chest, letting the tears flow.

RUSSELL TURNED INTO the narrow alleyway leading down the side of Tony Lagorio's restaurant—a dark building on the corner of the block, just off Dean Street. He knocked twice on the side door and waited.

There had been no point bringing Joe. It was going to be tough enough getting anything out of Tony without bringing a puppy into the dog pit. Besides, Russell was still reeling from what had happened to Chris, and needed a break from the relentless questions.

He knew his former colleagues on the force would let the case fade into obscurity as they had with so many similar attacks over the years. Gay-bashing wasn't exactly a high priority for any of them—quite often the police were the worst perpetrators of those kinds of attacks themselves. As Russell knew only too well, having been caught out in a sting set up by his own colleagues.

A young man, tight jeans, torn pocket, had approached him outside a club. They'd chatted briefly, and the guy had offered sex, saying they should go back to his place. Russell should have known it was a set up—no one ever propositioned him.

But booze and loneliness meant he'd fallen for it, and just around the corner they'd been surrounded by two other guys who identified themselves as coppers and arrested Russell on a charge of opportuning. An old, rarely used charge from the fifties which had been designed to stop men hanging round stage doors and harassing the showgirls.

Russell knew that Skinner had set it up. He was yet to prove it, but he knew. As far as detectives like Skinner were concerned, if you were gay and out, you brought any trouble you got on yourself. Skinner wouldn't break a sweat trying to solve Chris's murder.

He also knew that Skinner would blow a gasket if he knew Russell was looking into what had happened, which made him all the more determined to do something. If he found Chris's real killer, and proved it was more than just a random attack, it would make Skinner look bad. And nothing would make Russell happier than damaging Skinner's reputation.

One day, Russell would find a way to pay Skinner back properly. For now, he was more interested in what had happened to Chris.

He knocked again, harder this time, and finally heard the sound of bolts sliding back heavily on the inside of the door. The door opened a crack—chain still in place.

"What d'you want?"

"I'm here to see Tony," Russell said.

"Tony don't see no one without an appointment—least of all the pigs." His cockney accent was nasal and whiny, the voice of a natural-born scrapper.

"Tell him I'm here about Chris Sexton," said Russell, his foot stopping the door from closing. "The designer," he added.

"Remove your foot, or I will break your leg and remove it for you."

The way he pronounced every syllable of every word expressed such clear violent intent that Russell did as he was told. The door slammed shut, bolts sliding home again. He waited as footsteps thudded away.

A rusty fire escape ladder hung above his head, too far out of reach for him to grab. He would just have to wait, and hope Tony agreed to see him.

The door to the pub opposite opened, a burst of Jimmy Sommerville's distinctive falsetto following a couple of lads out onto the street—skinny boys in leather and denim, cropped T-shirts, shaved heads. They laughed, jostling each other as they passed the mouth of the alleyway, neither of them looking in.

Tony's building was three storeys high. The restaurant occupied all of the ground floor, and Russell could see lights burning on the second. He knew the place well—he'd tried to get a warrant to search it a number of times. Never succeeded.

TAINTED LOVE

There were two tables in the restaurant at which no one could eat without an invitation, and invitations were like hen's teeth. Both were empty today. The rest of the tables were open to anyone with enough cash to pay over-inflated prices for underwhelming food. The old-fashioned Italian was little more than a front for Tony's other interests, he didn't need it to turn a profit.

Try as he might during his time as a detective with the Metropolitan Police, Russell had never been able to make any charges stick to Tony Lagorio, and it still annoyed him. Probably almost as much as each of his attempts to do so had annoyed Tony.

There had been such bad blood between the two of them over the years that Russell felt uncharacteristically nervous about seeing him again.

The last time they'd seen each other, Tony had been striding out of a holding cell that Russell had put him in, with a smile on his lips, a threat in his eyes, and an expensive lawyer at his side.

Russell had always wondered if Tony hadn't deliberately sought Chris out and offered him a deal too good to be true on that loan, before turning the screws on him, simply to get back at Russell for one arrest too many.

He heard the footsteps returning. Not in any kind of hurry. Bolts shifted again. The chain was removed, and the door opened to reveal a short, broad man with one gold tooth in an otherwise solidly white, horribly chilling smile.

"You've got five minutes," he snarled.

Russell threw him a fake smile and headed up the stairs towards the rooms above. He followed the smell of cigar smoke down the dank corridor and into the large office overlooking the busy street below.

Tony Lagorio stood in front of one of the windows, gazing down at the street, his back to the room, confident to the point of arrogance.

A cigar smouldered in an ashtray on the desk in front of the window, and his chair was still gently swivelling—he'd only stood up for effect.

"So, the kid thinks he can send messengers now, does he?"

Russell stepped into the room and closed the door. He didn't want any of Tony's goons jumping him from behind.

"Chris is dead, Tony," he said. "That's why I'm here."

The Lizard turned around the moment Russell started talking. "You?"

Russell forced a smile, toothy and insincere. "Me."

"I thought you'd been... retired."

Russell sat down, uninvited, in one of the chairs facing Tony's oversized oak desk.

"Let's call this a personal visit," Russell said, forcing himself to speak slowly, play Tony at his own game. "Chris was a very dear friend, as you know."

Tony raised an eyebrow.

"I hear you went to find him in the club," Russell said. "On the night he died. Thought you might be able to tell me what was going on between you two?"

Russell may have arrested Tony Lagorio a handful of times in the past, but he'd never seen him look as shocked as he did right now.

The big man sat down, rubbed his spade-like palms over his face and stared at Russell for a moment.

"Dead?" he asked, finally.

"I'm afraid so," Russell replied. "We found him in the early hours of Saturday morning, in the doorway of our flat."

"I'm sorry," Tony said. "Truly."

And Russell felt that he meant it. He could see the big man's mind working, trying to process the information. The Lizard was no stranger to sudden deaths, but something about the news had shocked him.

"So," Russell pushed, not wanting to give Tony time to recover his composure. "You can imagine my surprise to hear that you, of all people, had gone to find him in the club that night. What did you have to say to him that couldn't wait for a phonecall in the morning?"

"That's none of your business," Tony said.

"I'm making it my business," Russell countered. "And you know how annoying I can be when I start doing that."

Tony smirked, relit the cigar and leaned back in his chair. He wasn't bothered. Was Russell losing his edge? Too long out of the job, and not even the leverage of the badge to force the pretence of respect. *Plough on, quickly.*

"From what I hear, you two had a bit of a disagreement. Made him change his plans for the night. And then he turns up dead. There are witnesses who saw you threaten him, Tony."

"Witnesses? What witnesses?"

"Not important. Just tell me what you said. Why did he leave the club in such a hurry?"

Tony leaned back in his chair, fingers steepled in front of his chest, cigar dangling from his fat lips. He sniffed. Blew out a cloud of smoke.

"I'll cut you some slack," he said quietly, "because, despite everything, I can see you were a good cop, and I don't agree with what they did to you on the force. What you do in your own life shouldn't hold any interest for anyone else. So long as you're not hurting anyone, right?"

An ironic sentiment from a man who'd spent most of his life having people hurt. Russell said nothing.

"And, regardless of what you think," Tony continued, "I liked the kid. I would have liked him a whole lot more if he'd paid his debts on time, and not made me chase him round the city, but them's the breaks. We got there in the end."

Russell sat forward. Tony stubbed out the cigar.

"So here's the deal," Tony said, leaning back in his chair. "We had an arrangement. A service arrangement, if you will."

"Meaning?"

"I have a couple of high-end clients who enjoy a discreet evening in the company of a nice, willing young man."

"You pimped him out?"

"Well, that makes it sound very crass. No. I made some introductions, and I let him take it from there. What he actually did with the guys was none of my business."

It was Russell's turn to get over the shock. He had no idea Chris had been working as an escort, but he supposed it made sense. He should have guessed when Chris suddenly seemed to be flush with cash all the time. He forced himself to keep listening to Tony's reply, he could ponder the rest later.

"Sometimes, I asked him to get me a little information while he was working. Pillow talk is a valuable commodity. And I paid him well for the information he got. It was a business arrangement. Purely financial. I knew he'd done worse before. Hell, he even offered to do me once, back in the day, if I let the debt slide. I told him no thanks." He laughed, as though the thought was ridiculous. "I was *helping* him," Tony protested, when he realised Russell didn't share the joke. "At first, he needed a way to pay back what he owed me. I just hooked him up with some clients who could pay properly for what he had to offer. He was a popular kid. We soon figured out that people would share secrets with him. But that was his idea. He came to me the first time, with information to sell."

"Okay," Russell said, "I get all that. I don't like it, but I get it. It doesn't explain why you were threatening him in the club on Friday though, does it?"

TAINTED LOVE

"I don't have to explain myself to you."

"Oh, come on, Tony," Russell said, leaning forward, elbows on knees. "I know you've probably got more friends on the force than I ever did, but you know what they think of kids like Chris. Do you really want to go through the hassle of having to explain what you were doing chasing him around a nightclub on a Friday night, making threats? On the same night he was brutally murdered in his own doorway? Even *your* friends might not be able to smooth that one over for you."

Tony held up his hands, the gesture more placatory than defensive.

"Hey, hold on there," he said. "I didn't hurt the kid. He was fine when I left him."

Russell stood up. He wasn't getting anywhere.

"You know what? The guy who's taken over from me on the force is eager to make a good impression. I'm sure he'll be very happy to claim a big scalp like yours on his first case. I don't know him well, but I'm sure he'll make time to listen to an old hand like me."

It was bullshit. Russell hadn't even been replaced on the force, and there was no way anyone in the department would bring in Tony Lagorio to answer for the death of a little gay boy. But, for now, Tony wasn't to know that, and Russell felt that he had just this one bluff to get closer to the truth.

"Fine. I'll level with you. I needed some information about a deal, and I needed it quick. Chris was supposed to be getting it for me, but he'd been avoiding me and I got tired of waiting, so I went down there to chivvy him along. He was a good kid, but he did get distracted easily."

"What information?"

"I'm not at liberty to say."

"He's dead, Tony," Russell said, exasperated. "Killed as he got home. If you know something, anything..."

"Whatever happened to him, I can tell you it was nothing to do with me. And that's the God's honest truth."

Tony's eyes flickered down to his watch. Whatever he knew, he wasn't about to share it with Russell. Tony shook his head, tired of this conversation, and pressed an intercom buzzer on his desk.

The door opened, and the gold-toothed man leered in.

"The gentleman is just leaving, Danny. Perhaps you could see him out."

Russell stood up to go. He wasn't going to get any more out of Tony today.

"I know you're a well-connected man," Russell said. "Ear to the ground and all that. So if you do hear anything, let me know, will you?"

"Oh, you'll be the first person I call."

He grinned at Russell, no humour there at all. As Russell headed through the door, Tony called after him.

"You know, this was probably all down to that fast mouth of his. Never could keep it shut. Looks like someone shut it for him. He was a good kid, but he was always going to end up on someone's bad side."

"I think you might be right, Tony," Russell said, an idea forming. "Chris knew a lot of secrets—but wasn't so great at keeping confidences. Like you say, he did have a fast mouth. Never could keep it shut when he'd had a drink. The things he's told me..."

Russell raised his eyebrows, smiling knowingly, then turned and walked out, not waiting to let Tony respond. It was becoming clear that Chris had been killed because he knew something that someone else wanted to keep secret. Who and what were still to be discovered, but he guessed Tony wanted that information too. Not enough to kill Chris for it, but enough to chase him down to the club and hassle him for it. Playing Tony at his own game was a gamble. He only hoped it would pay off.

RUSSELL SAT IN THE WINDOW of the small pub opposite Tony Lagorio's restaurant, nursing a pint that was rapidly going flat, and monitoring the comings and goings down the side alley.

He had left Tony half an hour ago with the distinct feeling that the burly gangster knew more than he was telling. Russell didn't really know what or who he was waiting for, but he had a hunch he should watch the place for a while and see who showed up.

He was just beginning to doubt his instincts, when he spotted a young man he recognised hurrying down the street towards the restaurant. Gavin Jones—Chris's business partner in the fashion label. Sharp suit, high-waisted pants, nice brogues, hair slicked in an immaculately precise side-parting.

Russell sat up straight, suddenly intrigued as Gavin walked straight past the alley and pushed open the door of the restaurant. He disappeared from sight for a moment, and then reappeared at a table in the window. One of the two invitation-only tables. He said something to the waiter who scuttled off, leaving Gavin alone to settle down.

Russell hadn't spent much time with Gavin. Chris rarely socialised with his business partner outside of work. He had seemed charming enough on the few occasions that Russell had met him. A little awkward and uptight though that was probably more down to his family background and private education than his personality.

Gavin came from a very wealthy family and, from the sound of it, had spent most of his life not living up to his father's expectations. It was one of the few things Russell had thought Gavin and Chris had in common—disappointed fathers.

Gavin looked up from his menu as a Bentley pulled up alongside the kerb. Tinted rear windows, personalised plates. *Speak of the devil.*

The driver in the car behind hooted and swerved around them, waving an insult as he passed. No reaction from the chauffeur of the Bentley.

The rear passenger door opened and Gavin's father stepped out. Russell recognised him from the launch party for Gavin and Chris's label, not to mention the countless newspaper articles about his various deals and scandals. A businessman, multi-millionaire, and one of the most arrogant and dismissive men Russell had ever met.

He crossed the street quickly, entered the restaurant and joined his son at the table in the window. Gavin stood as his father arrived, but there was no embrace, not even a handshake. No wonder the kid was uptight.

The waiter arrived with a bottle of water and filled their glasses, took an instruction from Gavin's father and hurried off. The conversation was one-sided. Gavin's head nodding sullenly as his father spoke, fast and firm, hands gesticulating fluidly.

The conversation stopped abruptly as Tony appeared at the table and sat down between them, elbows on the table, fat fingers interlaced. He looked flustered and unhappy.

Gavin slid a folder across the table towards him, saying something as Tony opened it and read the contents. Tony closed the folder, looked up at Gavin who shut up quickly as Tony threw the folder back at him, scattering papers over the floor around the table.

Gavin fumbled the papers back into the folder while his father got to his feet. Tony did the same and the two men stood face to face for a moment before Tony snarled something and left.

The waiter stepped forward, offered Gavin's father his coat, and escorted him to the door. The millionaire turned back in the doorway, shouted something at his son, waved a warning finger, and strode out into the street, exuding rage and frustration.

In no time, the Bentley appeared again, and he slipped into the back, closing the door as the car pulled back into the stream of traffic.

What was that all about?

Russell tore his eyes off the retreating car just in time to see another familiar figure slip into the alleyway up the side of the restaurant. He'd almost missed it. He'd allowed himself to get distracted.

He watched as they approached the door and looked back over their shoulder before knocking. The door opened quickly, and they slipped inside without another backward glance.

That's interesting, Russell thought. *What are you doing here?*

5.

JOE WOKE TO FIND early dawn light creeping through the open window. He'd obviously slept through the night, though it had been a restless sleep, filled with half-forgotten dreams and disquieted voices.

Waking up on Chris's bed, he wondered if the whole thing had been a horrible nightmare, but when he saw Chris's jacket crumpled beneath him, that awful reality flooded back.

He walked into the kitchen to find Russell sitting at the small table, a sheet of paper in front of him, head bent and scribbling with a cigarette burning between his fingers. He looked up as Joe came in.

"Ah, you're up," Russell said.

"Yeah, sorry, I passed out. Must have slept through. Tea?"

"I've got one, thanks," Russell said, tapping his mug with the end of his pen.

Joe flicked the kettle on and craned over Russell's shoulder to see what he was writing. Meaningless doodling for the most part.

"Did you manage to get any sleep?" Joe asked.

"Enough."

Russell didn't look like he'd slept at all. His thinning hair was dishevelled, his eyes baggy and red, his shoulders slumped. Joe brought his mug back to the table and sat down heavily.

"Did you talk to him? This Lizard guy?" he asked.

"I did," Russell sighed, and took a drag of his cigarette, stubbing the half-smoked tab out in the ashtray and standing up to turn the radio off, drowning out yet another report of the miners' strike.

He placed the ashtray beside the sink, his movements precise and controlled. Russell liked things in the flat to be *just-so*, Chris had told Joe before he'd brought him home. "He's a neat freak," he'd said. "So don't move anything unless it's in my room. And don't leave your stuff lying around. He hates that."

Joe watched Russell pick up a dish cloth from the sink, wring it out, and wipe an already clean surface. Fast at first, gradually slowing until the cloth lay still beneath his clenched fist. Something was clearly bothering him.

"Well, what did he say?" Joe asked.

"Hmm?"

Russell turned from the sink and looked at Joe as though he'd almost forgotten he was there.

"It's what he didn't say that's more intriguing," he said, shaking his head.

He sounded distant, like he was trying to pull together a web of random, fleeting thoughts. Nodding to himself, he sat down again, lifted another cigarette from the packet and lit it, drawing the smoke in through tight lips. He offered the packet to Joe.

"No thanks," Joe said. "I don't really smoke."

"Well, aren't you the good boy?"

"Hardly," Joe said. But he was, if truth be told.

Russell blew a long stream of smoke out the side of his mouth, standing up again and pacing. Restless. Anxious. He stopped at the sink, staring out of the window, and seemed to freeze again.

"Did he say why he'd been to see Chris? Did he know where he went after he left the club?"

"Slow down," Russell said, tersely. "I'm trying to get everything straight in my head."

Joe took a sip of his tea and waited. He was beginning to figure out how Russell ticked, and too many questions when he was thinking definitely seemed to wind him up.

"He said he'd been paying Chris to get information for him," Russell said, eventually. "But apparently Chris was delaying, so he went to the club to chivvy him along."

"D'you think he killed Chris?"

Russell looked up at him.

"No. What happened to Chris was not Tony's style. But he knows where Chris went when he left the club."

"Where?"

"He wouldn't tell me."

"Great. So what now?"

"We go back over everything we know."

"Which is what?"

"Okay," Russell said, stretching. "Chris was struggling to make something of the business when Gavin stepped in. I saw Gavin, by the way, at Tony's restaurant, but we'll come back to that."

Joe leaned back, intrigued, as Russell continued.

"So Gavin stepped in as partner, with Daddy's money behind him and, like every other fool—present company included—promptly fell in love with him. But Chris refused to give him a managing share and, to keep his own half of the business, he decided to borrow the money from Tony."

"A known gangster," said Joe.

"Exactly. But then he struggled to pay it back, and Tony doesn't like waiting, so Tony offered him a different kind of opportunity."

"What?"

Russell hesitated to tell him.

"What?" Joe repeated.

"He said that he and had Chris had an arrangement," he sighed. "There were a couple of high-end clients, who apparently paid well for Chris's services."

"Services?" Joe spluttered. "You mean he was...?"

"Sleeping with guys for cash, yes," Russell confirmed.

"But—" Joe hesitated. "What, so this Lizard guy was his pimp?"

"I don't think he'd take kindly to that label. He says he just made a couple of introductions to clients who paid well for a high level of secrecy. It meant Chris could pay him back quicker. He doesn't know, or care, what they did together."

"So your detective friend was right," Joe said, feeling that another part of the friend he'd known had just been stripped away from his memory. "Chris *was* just a stupid rent boy."

He felt so angry with Chris. Had everything about him been a lie? Surely he hadn't needed to turn to prostitution to make money? He could have just asked. Joe would have helped him somehow. Then maybe he'd still be here.

Russell turned on him.

"No," he said. "Whatever he was doing, it wasn't as bad as you're imagining. You can't let this be how you remember him."

"But he could have asked if he needed money."

"He never would. You knew him. He had to be in control of everything. He always had a plan."

It was true. Chris would never have admitted to Joe that he was in trouble. He would never have asked for a handout. He would have been certain that he could solve his own problems without anyone else's help. He'd always been like that. It was one of the things Joe had loved so much about him.

"Besides, I think this was about more than just money," Russell said. "I should have known he was up to something, though."

"Why?"

"He came home this one time, about six months ago, really badly beaten—cracked ribs, broken jaw, the lot. He said he'd hooked up with some guy who'd turned nasty. I didn't press him for details. Maybe I should have."

"You think one of these clients beat him up?"

"I didn't know what he was doing at the time, obviously. But now... Well, maybe. You see, two days after he got beaten, a cheque turned up in the post for five hundred quid. He tore it up. Wouldn't talk about it. But the whole incident changed him. He seemed angrier after that, but also more driven."

"But if he was so desperate for money, why did he tear the cheque up?"

"He said it wasn't enough. Said he was going to make him pay properly."

"What did he mean? Make who pay?"

"No idea. Like I said, he wouldn't talk about it, and I didn't pry. The wounds healed, the bruises faded, and he seemed to be getting back on his feet."

"If he'd paid Tony off," Joe mused. "Why was he still seeing these guys?"

"Tony said they'd come to an arrangement where he would pay Chris for information he got from his clients. Pillow talk. Said Chris had a gift for getting people to share their secrets."

"So that's where all the money was coming from?"

"I'm not sure. It doesn't add up," Russell said, getting up again and pacing the floor. "I assumed the business was doing better, with all their new clients. But the amount he was spending—he paid back all the rent he'd missed in one hit, bought designer clothes, things for the flat. Unless the information he was getting was like gold dust, even Tony wouldn't be that generous. There's something we're missing."

"And Tony wouldn't tell you who Chris went to see the night he was killed?" Joe asked.

"Nope. There's bad blood between us. He's hardly likely to share his business secrets. All he said was that Chris was supposed to give him some important information, and he hadn't done it yet, so Tony went to hurry him up."

"So, where do we go from here?"

"Listen," Russell sighed, looking awkward. "I've been thinking about this, and… well, don't take it the wrong way, but I never was much of a team player, and I'm not looking for a new partner. I'm going to find out what happened to Chris, but I don't think you should get involved. It's just too dangerous."

Joe wasn't about to be shut out.

"Well, I *am* involved, whether you like it or not, and I'm not going anywhere until I find out what happened. He was my best friend. I loved him."

Joe saw a glimmer of resigned understanding cross Russell's face. A sudden thought struck him.

"Wait there," he said, excitedly, dashing off to Chris's room, and coming back with the little black diary.

"What's this?" Russell asked.

"I found it in one of Chris's drawers. It's a diary from last year, but look, it's a list of appointments or something. Some of them repeat regularly."

Russell flicked through the little book, back and forth through the pages.

"It's all just initials," he said. "It could be anything. Something to do with his label. His suppliers, maybe. Or new orders."

"I know, but it could also be a list of these clients Tony was talking about. The ones who didn't want their names used. When was it he got beaten up? Can you remember?"

Joe took the diary back, holding it eagerly. Russell bit his lip, thinking.

"It was just after my birthday. Must have been the Friday because we were all going to go out on the Saturday and he couldn't come. The cheque came on the Monday."

"So?" Joe prompted, ready.

"Friday the tenth of August."

Joe flicked through the pages until he found the right date.

"Huh," he said.

"What?"

Joe paged back through the diary to check. "MJ. Underlined twice. Hang on."

He turned back through the pages quickly, searching for the entry he'd seen earlier.

"See here?" he asked excitedly, holding the diary out to Russell. "He had this X marked in. And X was becoming more regular, see? And then, on this day, he's crossed out the X and put MJ instead. But look at that exclamation mark. Does that mean he figured out who X was? Because if so, then the next time he saw him was the night he got beaten up."

"Now that is interesting," said Russell, sounding more animated.

"But who the hell is MJ?" Joe asked.

"That's what we're going to find out."

They both stared at the diary. Was this a break, or another dead end?

AFTER A SOLID BREAKFAST, a couple of strong coffees, a shower and a change of clothes, Joe was ready to hit the streets.

The headlines on the stands outside the newsagent shouted that almost half of the striking miners had just gone back to work. It seemed the strike might finally be coming to an end.

TAINTED LOVE

Joe picked up a copy of one of the papers, determined to read it at some point in the day. He'd been following the miners' strike since the very beginning, and even more so since a small group of gays and lesbians from London had started going down to the picket lines with supplies and support.

It had been the only time he'd sent a newspaper cutting back to his sister, whose husband was a miner. *Stick that up your chuff, Deborah. Gays are good people too.* Unsurprisingly, she hadn't mentioned receiving it.

Joe and Russell had agreed to split forces, with Joe heading over to the fashion studio to have a chat with Chris's business partner, Gavin.

Chris had been so excited about a couple of big clients they had just secured, but he also mentioned that he and Gavin had been arguing a lot about the direction that their business should take.

If Chris's closest friends didn't know what had been going on in his life, did his business partner? How much of Chris's illicit income had gone back into the business? And did Gavin know about any of it?

At the moment it felt like they had lots of little leads, but nothing concrete. They had agreed to pull at every thread that was still hanging loose, and see what unravelled. One of them would lead to Chris's killer.

Joe remembered being particularly underwhelmed by Chris's business partner when he'd met him last year. In fact, he was struggling to remember what Gavin looked like. Still—hopefully he'd be able to tell them what Chris had been like to work with recently, and whether anyone had been bothering him at work.

"What are you going to do then?" Joe had asked. "While I'm talking to Gavin?"

"I have another couple of leads to follow up," Russell had said, dismissively. "Let's catch up at the Red Lion later, I want to talk to Paul again too."

Joe had a feeling that Russell had been trying to get him out the way. Russell had been distracted all morning, and Joe doubted he'd gone to bed at all. Something about that meeting with Tony Lagorio had disturbed him, and Joe had decided to engage in a little covert surveillance of his own, to see what was really going on.

He concealed himself in the alley where he'd found Patty hiding on the night Chris died. It was damp and smelled of piss, but it was dark and kept him hidden while he watched the front door of Russell's flat.

RUSSELL HAD A REASON for wanting Joe to go alone to see Gavin, but he didn't want to tell him about it yet. The figure he'd seen going into the alleyway had got him thinking and, slowly but surely, the old synapses were beginning to fire again.

With Joe safely out of the door and on his way, Russell sat down to wait—a fresh pot of coffee on the table, and a cigarette in hand. He'd deliberately planted a seed with Tony, suggesting that Chris might have shared a secret or two with him, hoping that the seed would take hold and Tony would scurry to get those secrets for himself.

The thing that had been disturbing him the most was the missing roll of film from Chris's camera. Whoever had come for him had wanted those photographs, and they'd been willing to kill for them.

While he didn't believe Tony had killed Chris, he did think that the big man knew exactly where Chris had been and what he'd been up to. Either way, he was sure Tony would act; and as soon as he'd seen the person entering the alleyway, he knew how it would play out.

He didn't have to wait long before there was a knock at the door, loud and official. Sure enough, when he opened the door, Detective Skinner was on the doorstep. Uncharacteristically, he'd come alone.

"I thought it'd be you he sent," Russell said, enjoying the frown that crossed Skinner's face. "Forget something, did you?"

Russell turned away from the door, heading back up the stairs, and felt Skinner hesitate for just a moment. He'd caught him off guard, and that made Russell happier than it should.

He'd known Skinner was corrupt for years, but he'd never been able to prove it. He was playing a dangerous game, given what had already happened to Chris, and knowing that Skinner was almost single-handedly responsible for him losing his job in the force, but he was onto something here, and if there was even the smallest chance he could find Chris's killer while exposing Skinner for the useless waste of skin he was, then he was going to grab it with both hands.

"Come on in, Detective," he said, lacing the man's job title with sarcasm.

Skinner followed him up the stairs and into the kitchen. Russell sat down, affecting the most relaxed pose he could muster.

"Coffee? I've just made a fresh pot," he offered, with obviously false bonhomie.

"No thanks, I'm not staying." Skinner said, standing in the doorway, as though entering the room would cause him to spontaneously combust.

"Found the killer yet?" Russell asked. "Got any promising leads?"

Russell was goading him and he was enjoying it. Skinner was not.

"I need to look through Mr Sexton's belongings," Skinner said.

"Sure," Russell said. "Show me your warrant and I'll take you through."

Skinner stood there, seething. Of course there was no warrant.

"I don't need a warrant."

"I'm afraid you do if you want to search my house," Russell smiled. "I'd have thought you'd know that. Man of your experience."

Skinner said nothing.

"What's the matter? Cat got your tongue?"

It was exactly the question Skinner had asked him the day Russell had been suspended—making sure he knew who had set him up for the fall.

"What did Tony send you back to look for, then?" Russell asked, cutting to the chase. "Documents? Lists? Photographs?"

"What?"

Too late. Russell had seen the flinch.

"The Lizard," Russell said. "That *was* you I saw visiting him yesterday, wasn't it? Funny, I thought, how you turned up just after I alerted him to the idea that Chris might have held some evidence back from him. Evidence that you didn't manage to take away when you examined the scene. Evidence that Tony clearly wanted."

"I don't know what you're talking about," Skinner stammered.

"Ah, it was ever thus," Russell teased.

Skinner stepped into the kitchen, jaw clenched, eyes black.

"Yes, I was there," he said. "I was simply pursuing a line of enquiry. Mr Lagorio was a known associate of the victim, and I had some questions for him."

"Oh, so you know he was one of the last people to see Chris alive, then? Arguing in the club, in front of all of those witnesses.

Did he tell you how he'd been using Chris to steal information from his rivals?"

Each question was like a punch in the gut.

"That's always been your problem, Skinner," Russell tutted. "You've never asked the right questions. Never enjoyed the actual nitty gritty of detective work. It can be quite rewarding, you know? If done properly."

Skinner's lip curled. Russell stood up, sensing he might make a break for Chris's room. He leaned in the doorway to the corridor, coffee in hand.

"Unless you come back with a warrant, you're not coming in again."

"I could have you for obstructing an investigation."

"No, you couldn't," Russell replied. "We both know I'm right. So off you pop and do your paperwork like a good boy because you won't get anywhere in this house without it."

"I'll be back," Skinner said, realising he wasn't going to get past.

"Well you'd better be quick," Russell called, as Skinner stomped down the stairs. "Because my interest is already piqued, and you know what I'm like when I get my teeth into something. You wouldn't want me to beat you to it, would you?"

He didn't breathe until the door slammed and Skinner was gone. He still had so much to figure out. But it was all starting to take shape.

JOE DIDN'T LEAVE the alleyway until after Skinner stormed out of the flat, slamming the door. He'd half-debated nipping back up to the flat while Skinner was in there, just to make sure nothing bad was happening. He didn't trust that snivelling so-called detective, but he knew by now that Russell could handle himself. Still, he was surprised how protective he felt of Chris's former flatmate.

Having seen Russell come to the window to watch his old colleague leave, Joe slipped out of the alleyway and followed Skinner out of the square at a safe enough distance. When the detective ducked down into the underground station, Joe doubled back to get on with the task in hand—Gavin. He would talk to Russell about Skinner later.

CHRIS AND GAVIN'S STUDIO was, in fact, just a big-windowed room above a row of shops. An old lift ran a creaking service between the ground floor and the studio, but Joe took the stairs. He had never been good in confined spaces anyway, and the clunking and grinding of gears as the lift rolled up had given him palpitations the first and only time he'd used it.

As Joe approached the studio doors, a growing hum of animated conversation rose from within. It sounded like a party. He knocked, but there was no reply.

Joe pushed the door open, and the hum died quickly as everyone turned to look at him. His was not a face any of them recognised, so back to their conversations they went.

He scanned the room, noticing a few famous faces, people that he recognised from Chris's wall at the flat, or from recent episodes of Top of the Pops—clients, so-called friends, social vultures scavenging on the bones left behind.

Joe almost walked out again, but he had already spotted Gavin. As soon as Chris's business partner saw him, he waved, cutting his way through the room.

"It's you, isn't it?" he said, looking Joe up and down. "Chris's friend from..." he waved his hand, dismissively.

"School," Joe filled in. "Joe."

"Of course," Gavin said, with no hint of recognition.

Too distracted by all the celebrities in the room, Gavin waved casually at a mid-range pop star on the other side of the room that Joe vaguely recognised—eyeliner, earrings and a trademark quirky hat being the defining features.

"Is this a bad time?" Joe asked.

Gavin rolled his eyes dramatically, head tilted. Camper than Joe remembered him.

"People have just been turning up all day, darling. Apparently they all just want to feel closer to Chris. They're all putting their name down for the new line. Now they know it'll be his last."

Gavin didn't sound too put out by the new crowd of celebrity punters. He stared longingly at the gathered group, keen to get back to any potential orders.

"Vultures," Joe muttered.

"What?" Gavin snapped back into the conversation. "Don't knock it. Chris has finally managed to turn himself into the overnight success he always claimed to be."

"Is there somewhere more private we can talk?" Joe asked, feeling annoyed at Gavin's distracted nonchalance.

"Oh God, really? Right now?" Gavin huffed. "I mean, the studio is heaving. Can't it wait?"

"No. It can't bloody wait. This wasn't some publicity stunt. Chris was murdered. I'd have thought you'd be more upset." Joe snapped.

"I really haven't got time for this," Gavin said, trying to block Joe's entry to the room. "I've got clients to attend to."

"Chris told me you'd been arguing about the new line," Joe blurted. "He said you hated his designs. Thought they looked cheap and nasty."

Joe had said the last part in a loud enough voice for Gavin to suddenly decide that this conversation would be best pursued out of earshot of the eager fashionistas.

Gavin hurried them both into the small office, furnished simply with two uncluttered desks and a designer's easel covered in sketches and fabric samples. Chris's distinctive, artistic writing, sketches and colour swatches covered the board.

Joe felt immediately drawn to it, crossing the room to get a closer look, his hand hovering over the board.

"Right," Gavin said, closing the door. "Let's make this quick."

"What the hell is wrong with you?" Joe snapped, unable to bite his tongue any longer.

Gavin looked taken aback.

"Don't you care that Chris is dead?"

"Of course I care," Gavin said, "But, unlike Chris, I don't display my emotions in front of the clients. I still have a business to run."

"So, what's been going on?" Joe asked. "Why had you been fighting so much?"

"We didn't fight. I mean, of course we *argued* all the time—we're fiery, creative people, darling. We had creative differences."

"The way Chris told it, you could barely be in the same room as one another," Joe said.

"Well, he's always been prone to exaggeration," Gavin snapped. "We argued often, but only because we're both passionate about making the label a success. The problem was, Chris just wouldn't listen to anyone else. He had to be in control, he always knew best."

Joe was about to ask another question when he remembered Russell's advice—let the silence breathe. Don't lead him. Let him fill in the gaps for you.

Joe angled himself towards the design board and ran his fingers over the sketches there.

Chris had told him he thought Gavin was jealous. People in the industry had begun whispering that Chris was the real design genius behind the label. Gavin's lip curled ever so slightly as Joe's fingers traced the pencil lines.

"I mean, look at these new designs," Gavin said, bitterly. "They're just derivative crap. We're supposed to be throwing modern twists on classic styles, not pandering to the overnight whims of plastic pop stars."

"You seem quite happy to take their money though," Joe said, nodding towards those very pop stars outside the room.

"Well, that lot out there wouldn't know high fashion if it kicked them in the arse," Gavin snapped. "They're only here because Chris is dead and they all want a piece of him. It's like *The Emperor's New Clothes*."

"You don't seem that upset that your business partner was murdered," Joe said bitterly, stepping closer to Gavin.

"Of course I'm upset," Gavin spluttered. "But that doesn't mean I have to suddenly change my mind about the designs, does it? Or about the way he'd been behaving?"

"No," said Joe, picking up a pile of sketches from Gavin's desk and thumbing through them. "But I suppose it does mean you can take the credit for the success of the business without being challenged, doesn't it?"

Gavin snatched the sketches from him and placed them face down on his desk.

"I haven't got time for this," he said. "I'm truly sorry you've lost your friend. But I have to move on with my business. He caused me enough trouble when he was alive, and I'm damned if I'm going to let him keep doing it now he's dead."

He opened the door, waiting expectantly for Joe to file out. Joe didn't move.

"You also argued about money," Joe said.

"Always," Gavin said, dismissively. "Chris wasn't good with money."

That was an understatement.

"From what I heard," Joe said. "You had a huge fight on the morning he died. What about?"

"Who told you that?" Gavin asked, surprised. Joe had hit a nerve there.

"Chris did. He told me you were trying to kick him out of the company."

"Buy him out, not kick him out," Gavin said wearily. "It's simple enough. I didn't trust him. I couldn't be in business with him any more."

"But you wanted to keep the label? Trade on *his* name," Joe hadn't meant it to sound so spiteful.

"It's *my* name too."

Gavin shut the door again, a little too hard. Joe was getting to him. It must have been difficult being in the shadow of a tour de force like Chris. Gavin was probably the backbone of the business, which would have made him all but invisible compared to Chris.

"Chris was a liability. I just couldn't work with him. So I offered to buy him out. He said he'd see me in court."

Joe smiled to himself. It sounded just like Chris. Volatile, dramatic and unrealistic.

"It's not funny," Gavin snapped. Joe's smile dropped.

"So what will you do now?" Joe asked.

"I'll launch a new line in the spring," Gavin said. "I have a new investor wanting to buy into the business. I can finally move to a bigger studio and build the label properly."

"That was quick," Joe said.

"I've been working on the deal for months," Gavin replied. "That's what Chris and I fought about that morning. I had letters from the lawyers. They'd found a way that I could legally remove him from the business, but keep the name. Chris was livid, but it was the only condition my new investor had: the business had to come *without* Chris."

Joe was shocked. Chris had only hinted at a split with Gavin, he hadn't said anything about the relationship being this bad. Why hadn't Chris told him?

They had spent the whole evening getting ready to go out, chatting about work and the future, and Chris had been in great spirits. He'd had to go off and do some work earlier in the afternoon but, even then, he'd seemed pretty happy about it. And yet, he had been on the brink of losing his business—forced out by his partner and a bunch of lawyers. It would have destroyed him, and he didn't let on at all.

"But this was his passion," Joe said, indicating the studio. "His dream. He wouldn't just roll over and let you take it all away."

"Chris was obsessed with this grotty little attic, but it's hardly the image we... *I* want to project. I offered to buy him out. He could stay here and set up again on his own, with all this."

He waved his hand dismissively at the designs on the board.

Joe remembered coming to the studio on the day Chris had first signed the lease. Chris had been giddy with excitement. It was small and shabby, but it was perfect for the little collective he'd set up with a couple of college friends. There had been three designers crammed in here back then, and Gavin hadn't been one of them.

"What happened to the others?" Joe asked. "I thought the studio was supposed to be a collective."

Gavin laughed.

"That was all a load of hippy crap. Fashion is a cut-throat business, darling. Chris may have had the designs, but he had no idea how to sell them. He needed a business partner not a group of adoring fans and hangers-on."

Gavin fiddled with a sheaf of papers on the desk, absently tidying them into a neat pile.

"They all bailed quickly enough once SEXTON & JONES took off. Success breeds contempt, doesn't it? And Chris did like to shove his success in their faces a bit too often. I know he was your friend, but he was little more than a bully to most of us."

Much as he didn't want to admit it, Joe knew Gavin was right. Chris liked to be the centre of attention, adored by all, and he could be pretty bitchy if he felt threatened or unloved. Still, Joe didn't want to hear any of this from Gavin.

"But Chris seemed so excited about the new clients you had," Joe said.

"Yes, his new celebrity friends," Gavin sneered, rolling his eyes at the group outside the office. "I should have known he wouldn't be able to handle the success. Sure, he had talent and people liked his work, but in the end, he didn't really have what it took to run the business, and he hated the fact that I did."

Gavin looked at Joe, eyes hard. There was still so much anger and resentment about Chris. This must have been festering for a while.

"I think that's the real reason he wouldn't let me buy him out. Spite. He would rather ruin the label altogether than let me have it. That's why I had to go to the lawyers."

It was strange, Joe thought, how people's perceptions of Chris could be so wildly different. From Detective Skinner, to Paul, to Gavin—none of them saw Chris the way Joe had.

"In this game, your name—your reputation—is all there is," Gavin explained. "It doesn't matter how good the designs are if you can't deliver the product.

Gavin sighed, shoulders dropping.

"As soon as I offered to buy him out, Chris started doing everything he could to give the company a bad name: missing deadlines, showing up to meetings drunk, going off on protest marches when he should have been in here working. He was burning out. And he was pissing people off. I wasn't prepared to let him ruin the business."

"You seem awfully popular right now for a business on the brink of disaster," Joe said, indicating the throng outside the office window.

"They're shallow and vacuous," Gavin said. "Now that he's dead, he's some kind of saint. They can't order quickly enough. He'll become an overnight success."

"Or rather, you will," Joe sniped.

"Well, at least I earned it," Gavin replied. "I'm sorry, but dying is the best thing Chris has ever done for me, and I'm not going to pretend otherwise. Now, if you don't mind, I've got to get back to my clients."

JOE EMERGED ONTO the street from the side entrance, escaping the babble of voices and charged emotions. He should be shocked that Gavin was so vitriolic, but he could see that Chris had been putting his partner through the wringer recently.

There was obviously no love lost between Gavin and Chris towards the end of their relationship if Gavin had been forced to resort to lawyers and outside investors to get rid of a partner who seemed hell bent on running them both into the ground.

Yet again, Joe realised, this was just not the image he'd had of Chris. Had he really been so blinkered to his friend's true character? He hoped not.

Even in their last moments together, sitting in Chris's room, with Joe wearing one of his latest creations, Chris had been full of enthusiasm and excitement about his business. But thinking about it now, though, Chris had only ever referred to it as *his*. "My label. My designs. My customers." Joe hadn't once heard him mention Gavin.

It seemed like everyone Joe spoke to had some kind of axe to grind with his old friend. He'd always seemed so popular too. As the layers of Chris's life were being peeled away, Joe realised he was hanging on to an old impression of his dear friend, unwilling to believe that he had changed so much.

"Charming guy, huh?" Russell said, clapping a hand on Joe's shoulder. Joe jumped. "Sorry, didn't mean to scare you. How did it go with Gavin?"

"He'd obviously reached the end of his tether with Chris. And he didn't seem too upset about his death. He'd got the lawyers involved, apparently. He was going to force Chris out of the business. Did you know that?"

"Ouch. No, I didn't. There wouldn't have been much Chris could do to stop it, either, if he'd got the family lawyers involved."

Joe frowned.

"You know who his family is, right?" Russell asked.

"No," Joe replied. "Should I?"

"He's Gavin Melville-Jones. He dropped the Melville part to distance himself from the empire—make a name for himself. But he is happy to take Daddy's support when he needs it."

Joe looked blank.

"His dad's Nigel Melville-Jones. The property tycoon. Old money. Owns half of Mayfair. Always in the papers. Nasty piece of work."

"Don't think I've ever heard of him," Joe replied.

"The whole family are always in the news. The uncle's a Tory MP. There was a scandal a year or so ago to do with the two brothers colluding on something or other. Taxes, planning permissions... I can't remember now, but it was big at the time."

Joe shook his head. Obviously, he'd been too ensconced in his own provincial little life to notice.

"I just don't get it," Joe said. "How did someone like Gavin, from that kind of family, end up running a fashion label in a shitty Soho studio with Chris? I mean, I loved Chris, but he wasn't even the kind of person you'd trust with your beer, let alone your family money."

"You underestimate him," Russell smiled. "Chris was sharp. Canny. He knew what he was doing. And, my God, he could design clothes that people wanted to wear. And he could draw a crowd around him. Celebrities, musicians, all of them loved him."

"They're all up there now," Joe sneered, "fawning over the new collection. Gavin is seething that Chris is still managing to outshine him, even when he's dead."

They both walked on in silence, hit by another reminder of a fabulous life snuffed out too soon.

"So where do you think Chris was getting all this money from? Do you think he was still seeing these secret clients?" Joe asked.

"I think we should go and talk to Paul again," Russell said. "I got the feeling he's been doing a little more prying into Chris's secrets than he was letting on."

Joe agreed. He had sensed the jealous tone in Paul's voice too. And he still wasn't happy with Paul's explanation of why he'd been over at Chris's flat on the night he died, and why he'd run away when he'd seen Joe.

6.

THE RED LION WAS FULL, the windows steamed up. Smoke hung thick in the air. Clamouring voices vied for an audience.

"Blimey," Russell said, pushing the door open and squeezing his way through the bodies towards the bar with Joe following close behind. He hadn't seen the place this busy in years, not in the daytime, anyway.

"What's going on?" Russell asked the barman, finally reaching the front of the throng.

"They're all off on another protest in a while. Apparently the eviction notice has been served on the Campbell Centre. There's going to be a sit-in. It's a shame Chris isn't here, he'd have been the first to tie himself to the railings."

"You're not wrong there," Russell said. "Two pints please, Ron."

"Pride?"

"Sure."

"They'll be heading out in a few minutes," he said. "You'll be able to hear yourself think."

While Ron poured the pints, Russell scanned the bar, looking for Paul. He spotted him in a corner, laughing with a young guy in a fluorescent crop top. The laugh didn't reach his eyes though and, as though sensing he was being watched, Paul looked up and caught Russell's eye. The smile dropped away completely when he saw Joe there too.

Russell knew that Paul was smitten with Chris, and having Chris's oldest friend turn up on the scene, with all their easy camaraderie and long history, had been yet another challenge for Paul's already fragile ego.

Chris had always managed to surround himself with these adoring young men who would all end up vying with each other for his attention. He'd enjoyed the control of playing them off against each other, choosing his favourites like a general in Rome. Russell had pulled him up on it a couple of times, pointing out how hurtful it could be.

"Oh, come on, I'm just having fun," Chris had laughed. "They must all know they don't stand a chance. But it's so wonderful to be adored."

His flippant arrogance had been one of the only things that Russell hadn't liked about Chris. Though even that had begun to recede since that beating Chris had taken last year. Some of his cocky bravado had faded, and a more serious, pensive side had begun to show itself. He'd started to pay attention to the people around him, started having a conscience, socially and politically. Russell had felt he was actually starting to grow up.

Ron was right. Chris would have been leading the protest about the closure of the Campbell Centre. It had become a real mission of his to keep it open.

One of their close friends, Thomas Campbell—a former lecturer at the fashion school, and the guy who had introduced Chris to Russell when he found out his protégé had needed a room in London—had died of AIDS the previous year, and it had hit Chris a lot harder than Russell would have imagined.

Thomas wasn't the first of Russell's peers to fall victim to the awful illness, but he had been the first for Chris. When he died, he'd left his modest estate to the charity that had cared for him in his final year, and the charity had renamed themselves to the Campbell Centre in honour of his bequest.

Thomas's illness had brought out the side of Chris that others seldom saw. A kind, nurturing side; gentle and selfless. He had spent hours visiting Thomas as the disease stole more from him; and all the while, he had become more incensed that so little could be done for the victims of this terrible killer which hung over them all.

After Thomas had died, Chris had become a campaigner for better treatment of AIDS patients, and better care for the dying. It was a thankless task, and one that took a huge chunk of his physical and emotional strength.

So it was no wonder he had lost some of his passion for the fashion industry, or running the business, and even in his own welfare. He'd caught a glimpse of how unfair life could be, and it had eaten away at him almost as much as the disease had eaten away at Thomas.

Russell had sat up enough evenings listening to him rant about the Ministry of Health, the lack of care, the underlying homophobia which allowed so many to die unsupported. Chris had even taken to volunteering at the centre when he could, and he'd dragged Russell along a few times too.

He had changed in those last few months of his life. Russell wondered now if that change had been about more than Thomas's death alone. These secret clients, selling information to Tony, losing his business—it all must have weighed so heavy on him, and yet he said nothing.

"There you are, lads," Ron said, placing the beers on the bar and breaking into Russell's train of thought. "On the house. For Chris."

"Thanks, Ron," Russell said, and raised his glass to meet Joe's. "To Chris."

Joe smiled and clinked glasses with him.

"To Chris," he agreed.

Russell realised he was growing quite fond of Chris's friend. Despite the awful circumstances of the last few days, he saw that Joe was an intelligent, thoughtful young man, who could probably do with even the smallest bit of his old friend's self-confidence.

As they drank, a handsome, dark-haired young man, who looked like he needed both a good wash and a solid night's sleep, sidled up beside Joe and placed a kiss on his cheek. Joe turned quickly, and Russell saw him relax as soon as he recognised the lad.

"Luc," Joe said, sounding happy for the first time in days.

"I'm so sorry," Luc said. "I heard what happened to Chris. It's so terrible."

The guy's accent was as delightful as his face.

"Yes, it's been awful," Joe replied.

"I can't even imagine. Are you okay?"

Joe turned to look at Russell.

"Russell, this is Luc," he said, awkwardly. "I was with him on the night..." his voice faded.

"Nice to meet you, Luc," Russell said quickly. They all knew which night. "Excuse me a minute, will you? I'll be right back."

Russell headed through the now dissipating crowd, towards Paul and his friend. Having Joe suddenly distracted was a perfect excuse to talk to Paul alone. Given Paul's infatuation with Chris, and his obvious jealousy of the friendship Joe and Chris had shared, Russell guessed he'd get more out of him on his own.

"How're you holding up, Paul?" he asked, slipping himself into the corner between Paul and the guy in the neon crop top. The guy smiled a superficial, half-sneering smile, and slinked away, his style having been well and truly cramped.

"I'm okay," Paul replied, his voice heavy. "It's been a bit crazy, to be honest. I still can't believe it."

"Look," Russell said, guiding him further into the corner. "I've been asking around, trying to find out a bit more about what Chris had been up to. I wanted to run a few things by you?"

"Me?" He sounded defensive. "I thought you and the little school friend were the ones playing Cagney and Lacey."

"Nobody's playing anything, Paul." Russell snapped, voice louder than necessary. "We're just trying to find out what happened to our friend. It's not a competition. Chris is gone, and unless we do something, his killer will just walk away without ever being caught."

Paul leaned away from him nervously. Russell needed to calm down. These kids were so fragile. He took a deep breath.

"Now, I'm giving you the benefit of the doubt, because I know how much you loved Chris, but I'll tell you this for free: his mate over there was about to go to the police to tell them that he saw you running away from the scene with Chris's blood on your hands."

Paul looked shocked. His mouth goldfishing as he tried to come up with a reply.

"Do you think they'd give a shit about finding out the truth before charging you? Because, I can assure you, they wouldn't. They'd collar you without question and leave you in the slammer to take your chances with the rapists and the murderers."

Paul was trying to be strong, but Russell saw the tears welling in his eyes. They were all so young and naïve, he had to remind himself. He put his hand on Paul's arm.

"It's alright," he said. "I told him to hold off going to the police. I know you didn't hurt Chris."

He felt Paul's arm relax under his grip.

"But I also know there's something you're not telling me."

Paul shook his head in denial.

"I was a detective for ten years, Paul. And a cop on the beat for long enough before that. I heard what you said when we talked to you before, even if Joe didn't. You know something. You either tell me now, or we tell the police you were outside the house on the night he died and you can explain the whole lot to them. If they'll bother listening."

Paul sagged.

"Okay," he said, looking around the room as more people filed out of the door, the noise level diminishing by the minute. "He'd started being really distant and secretive. Not coming out when he said he was going to, lying about where he'd been. I guessed he was seeing someone, and I was jealous. I'm not proud of it, but I'd started following him."

Russell let him speak. He was fairly sure Paul hadn't hurt Chris, but the threat of telling the police he'd been there had been more than enough to open the floodgates of confession.

"Anyway, I followed him all the way to this big house up in Mayfair and I watched him go in. I waited outside. I wanted to know who he was visiting there because suddenly all the money he'd been throwing around recently started making sense. He'd got himself some kind of sugar daddy."

Or a rich client, Russell thought.

"I waited for about an hour, in the pissing rain, and when he came out, I saw the guy up at the window, watching him leave. I couldn't believe it."

"What? Who was it?"

"That MP. Robert Melville-Jones. The one they're all protesting about today. The one who's selling the house on the corner and closing down the Campbell Centre. He's Gavin's bloody uncle. And Chris said he hated them all. But I saw them kissing."

Russell's instincts began firing as more of the pieces slotted into place.

"Well, I ran after him," Paul continued. "Tackled him about it. I was raging. How could he even be in the same room as that prick? Eventually he told me what he'd been doing."

Russell took a swig of beer, letting Paul talk.

"Tony had got him into doing some high-end clients for money. He said it had helped him pay off his debt to Tony, but then he realised that it was easier than he thought. I think he had actually started enjoying it."

The bar was almost empty now, Russell leaned over to grab his beer and caught Joe's eye. Joe frowned, and Russell gave him a look which he hoped indicated that he should stay where he was and leave them to talk alone. A slight nod. Message understood. Joe turned back to his gorgeous Frenchman. Paul leaned back on the bar, in full flow.

"They were always these rich guys, who would pay extra for discretion," Paul said, unable to keep the sneer from his voice. "Like that bloody hypocrite MP. Chris said he didn't know who he was at first. It was only when he saw Melville-Jones at that first protest back in the summer that he figured it out. He challenged him the next time he saw him. Chris couldn't understand how he could be so duplicitous. Closing down that centre, stripping support from AIDS victims, and all the while he was gay himself. Anyway, Melville-Jones lost it. Beat him up really badly."

"Melville-Jones did that to him?"

Russell had seen the MP many times on the TV news. He didn't look like he could slap a backside with any kind of force, let alone break a young man's jaw.

"Apparently he was really scared that Chris would go to the papers about it. He totally flipped. But then he sent a cheque to say sorry."

"I remember," Russell said. "I didn't know it was from him though. Chris tore it up."

"Yes, because he said he didn't want his guilt money. But I got to thinking, well, just imagine how bad it would be for his career if it came out that he was gay, and that he was paying rent boys for sex."

Russell didn't need to imagine. That's exactly how his own career had been brought to an untimely end. Paul obviously realised what he'd just said.

"Oh Jesus, sorry," he said.

"Don't worry about it," Russell replied, downing another slug of his pint, putting the glass on the bar and wiping his mouth with the back of his hand.

He was trying to calm down, but he was furious. With Chris for being so stupid. With Paul for not saying anything sooner. And with himself for not guessing what had been going on right under his nose. He could have stopped Chris. Maybe he could even have saved him.

"Why didn't you say anything before?"

Paul looked down at his feet. There was something else he wasn't saying. Russell waited for it.

"Because I've been blackmailing Melville-Jones ever since I found out about the two of them," he mumbled. "And I think he killed Chris because of it."

"Oh Jesus Christ, Paul!"

Paul looked totally distraught. Russell could have swung for him.

"So, you decided to blackmail an MP," Russell sighed. "And not just any MP, one who's part of the wealthiest families in London, with power and control beyond your wildest dreams. And then, despite thinking that he'd killed Chris, you just sat on your hands and said nothing? Jesus Christ! Did Gavin know about any of this? His bloody uncle!"

"No," Paul said. "But Tony did. He's been trying to buy that corner plot on Frith Street from them. He's been paying Chris extra to get something on the family, looking for a way to drive the price down. But Chris wouldn't give him anything, because he didn't want him to buy the building and close the Campbell Centre. He said Robert had promised to block the deal, but then he'd gone back on his word. That's what Chris had gone to see him about that night. It's all my fault."

Paul broke down. Russell didn't console him. How could he have been so stupid? The Melville-Jones family had more influence and power than anyone could imagine. Why on earth did Paul think he'd be able to get one over on them? He took Paul's face and turned it to look at him.

"Have you told anyone else about this?"

"No," Paul replied.

"Good. Keep it that way."

"What are you going to do?" Paul asked, and Russell sensed he meant it as much about himself as about the information he'd just passed on.

"I'm going to get to the bottom of this whole mess," Russell said. "And put it right. You stay here. Don't go anywhere—and don't talk to anyone. Not even Ron. Okay?"

He turned back to the bar, drained his pint, and walked off, tapping Joe's shoulder on his way past.

"Come on," he said. "We've got to go."

Russell clocked Joe's wistful look as he walked away from Luc. Unsurprising, really—he *was* gorgeous.

"You going to see him again?"

"Would have been nice, but he's going back to France tomorrow. Everything okay?"

"Far from it—but hopefully it will be soon. I know where Chris went after the club."

JOE HAD LISTENED, RAPT, as Russell filled him in on the conversation with Paul. He'd found it hard enough to learn that

Chris had been selling himself for cash, and sharing illicit information with a notorious gangster, but had Chris known that Paul was blackmailing the same politician he'd been seeing? Joe couldn't help feeling that Paul's jealousy might have cost his friend his life.

Russell had told him to go back to the flat and go through all of Chris's stuff again, looking for anything to do with the Campbell Centre or the Melville-Jones family. He promised to meet him back there shortly—he was going to call in a few favours from an old friend at the station and see if he could find Melville-Jones's address.

Joe opened the front door, and took a deep breath before stepping into the hallway. The memory of what he'd seen there was still too vivid and fresh and, despite Russell having paid for a team of professional cleaners to clear away all traces of Chris's blood, he couldn't help feeling uneasy as he stepped over the black-and-white tiles and headed up the stairs.

He paused on the landing outside the door to the flat. The door was open. Just a crack. Joe leaned in and saw that the lock had been forced. His heart jumped. Someone had broken in. What if they were still in there?

He held his breath for a moment, listening for sounds from within. Nothing. Slowly he stepped forward, pushing the door open gently, wincing at the soft creak from the old hinges.

Inside, the flat smelled different. Something sweet and musky. *Cologne.* And he recognised it. Joe stuck close to the wall and made his way up the corridor. The kitchen was empty, tidy, exactly the way they'd left it.

He froze as a floorboard creaked beneath his foot. He heard another noise too, a rustling noise, from further down the corridor. There *was* still somebody in the house. And they were in Chris's bedroom.

He approached Chris's door carefully, casting around for something within reach that he could use as a weapon. Of course there was nothing.

He held on to the door frame while he slipped his shoe off. It might be ridiculous, but at least it was something.

He pushed the door open quietly, seeing a slim, tall man in a dark hooded sweatshirt leaning over Chris's desk, turning out the drawers.

"Hey," Joe protested, stepping closer, shoe raised, heel first, ready to strike.

The man turned quickly, face still concealed by the hood on his sweatshirt, and charged at Joe, punching him quick and hard, right in the nose.

The pain was exceptional. His vision filled with a starburst of pinprick lights as the man shouldered him aside and sprinted away.

Joe held his nose, trying to stem the sudden flow of blood and ease the pain, willing it not to be broken.

"JOE? ARE YOU OKAY?" Russell asked, finding him lying on the couch with a cold compress on the bridge of his nose. "What happened?"

Joe peeled the compress away, blinking through the pain.

"There was someone in the flat when I got home," he said, his voice thickened by his damaged nose. "In Chris's room."

"Who was it?"

He swung his legs round, trying to lever himself off the sofa.

"I don't know. He did this before I got a chance to look at him."

"What happened to your shoe?"

"I thought I could use it to defend myself."

"Maybe you need to stop wearing pumps," Russell laughed. Poor kid. "Stay still a bit."

Russell headed to the sink and ran a tea towel under the tap. Joe had done a good job of cleaning up his face, but Russell noticed that he'd managed to drip blood all the way across the kitchen floor.

"Thanks," Joe said, taking the cool cloth from Russell and wincing as he pressed it to his nose.

"You okay?" Russell asked, peering at the cut.

"Yeah, I don't think it's broken, but it hurts."

"Makes you look ever so butch though. You'll live."

Russell left him nursing his bruises and went to check the damage to the flat. The lounge had been overturned, sofa cushions on the floor, his record collection spilled over the carpet, some of it smashed, pictures knocked from shelves. A mess, but it looked more like deliberate destruction rather than a search.

"I'll get you some pain killers," he said, passing Joe again on his way to Chris's room. Joe groaned, slowly standing up.

Unlike the lounge, Chris's room was completely destroyed—the contents of every drawer and shelf strewn across the floor, the mattress slewed off the bed, chair overturned, wardrobe emptied.

They wouldn't have found what they were looking for, but they'd had a good look. Had Skinner come back while they were out? Or was someone else also searching the evidence that Chris had gathered?

Stepping into the room, Russell took in the destruction. He picked up the small chair and righted it in front of Chris's desk. So much chaos. And for what?

He noticed the newspaper front page pinned to the board with Chris's face, front and centre, finger raised, screaming at Robert Melville-Jones. The image had almost captured the moment when Chris had discovered who his client was. The moment that would eventually lead to his death.

The jigsaw was coming together in Russell's mind. He knew why Chris had been killed, he just needed to figure out who of the potential suspects had done it.

Russell carefully took the page off the board and carried it back through to the kitchen. He handed Joe a couple of pain killers and poured him a glass of water.

"Is anything missing?" Joe asked. "What were they looking for?"

"Tony has been trying to force a quick sale of the Frith Street property. Chris was supposed to be getting him information that would help him get an advantage. But he died before he could give it to Tony, if he had it at all. Turns out Tony's also got Skinner in his pocket. Skinner came round earlier wanting to search Chris's room, but I'd already seen him at Tony's when I went in to rattle Tony's cage, so I knew what Skinner was after when he came back here. Naturally, I told him to piss off. He obviously waited for us to go out and he came back. Sadly for them, Skinner was too late. Whoever killed Chris, took the evidence with them. It was all on his camera."

"Who?"

Russell laid the newspaper article on the table.

"I think *he* may have an idea," he said, tapping the image of the MP. "Robert Melville-Jones."

"MJ," Joe said. "From the diary. Our mysterious Mr X."

"That's my guess."

"So what do we do? Tell Detective Skinner?"

"After what he just did to your face? No. Besides, the family has too much influence. Without the right evidence, they'll just shut any accusation down. I say we go and talk to him ourselves."

Joe's finger traced over the image of Chris in the newspaper. He obviously missed his friend. Russell missed him too.

They'd both been so caught up in finding out what had happened to Chris, neither of them had mourned the friend they'd lost. Perhaps that would come later.

"Come on," Russell said. "Let's have a drink, let those painkillers take effect, and in the morning, we'll go have a chat with our local MP."

7

RUSSELL AND JOE WAITED outside the expensive townhouse in Mayfair as the sound of the doorbell faded. There was a light on upstairs, so they knew someone was home.

Russell had been determined to get here early, to catch Melville-Jones before he left for work, and he had cajoled a reluctant Joe out of bed with strong coffee and more painkillers.

Joe kept his coat bundled up around him, standing just behind Russell. This place looked so grand and he felt suddenly scruffy in his old jeans and duffle coat, with a brawler's cut across his nose and two developing black eyes.

The light in the hallway came on and the door opened until the safety chain stopped it. A man peered out through the crack, eyeing them suspiciously.

"Mr Melville-Jones?" Russell asked, though it was unmistakably him.

"Can I help?" he asked nervously.

"Russell Dixon. I wonder if we might have a word. We have some questions for you regarding your relationship with a Mr Christopher Sexton."

He sounded so official, Joe thought. Years of practice door-stepping suspects would give you that confidence. Joe saw the look of panic flash across the man's face.

"I'm late for work," he stammered.

"I'm sure you'd rather we did this in private, Mr Melville-Jones. Rather than here on the doorstep."

"You'll have to come back another time," his voice was faltering. There would be no other time.

"We have some rather sensitive," Russell paused for effect, holding up a brown envelope, "matters to discuss."

A sigh. The door closed. Russell looked back at Joe and winked. The old empty envelope trick had worked. The chain slid back and the door opened fully.

"Come in then," Melville-Jones said reluctantly.

He peered up and down the street behind them as they shuffled in. It must be tough, Joe thought, living your life in the public eye like he did, terrified that one day someone would share your darkest secrets with the world, just like Paul had threatened to do.

"Follow me," Melville-Jones said, brusquely.

They did. He led them up a wide hallway and into a dark wood-panelled study. A heavy desk dominated the room, a green glass desk lamp casting a pool of light on ist crimson leather inlaid surface. The walls were lined with shelves of old books, neatly stacked in matching volumes.

"What do you want?" he asked, showing Russell and Joe to a pair of high-backed leather chairs in front of the desk as he took his own seat behind it.

"We're looking into the circumstances surrounding Chris Sexton's murder," Russell said, his voice calm and assured but careful not to give the wrong impression. They couldn't actually say they were the police, after all.

"And what does that have to do with me?" Melville-Jones asked. His accent was old money, public school, Oxbridge. A man used to commanding others, but his voice was thin and reedy, and wobbled a little as he asked. He knew damn well what it had to do with him.

"I'm going to cut to the chase," Russell said, tapping the envelope on his knee, letting the MP imagine the contents. "We know that you were, to put it delicately, seeing Chris occasionally. Paying for certain services."

He let it hang in the air. Melville-Jones began to stammer an objection but Russell cut across him.

"We also know that another party had threatened to expose your relationship, and had been using that threat to extort money from you."

Melville-Jones slumped back in his chair, realising that, in fact, they did know everything.

"You don't understand," Melville-Jones began. Russell wasn't going to give him any slack at this stage in the questioning.

"Where were you on the night of Friday the fifteenth of February?" Russell asked.

"I was here," Melville-Jones stuttered. "But you can't possibly think I killed Chris?"

He sounded so outraged and hurt by the suggestion that, for just a moment, Joe wondered whether they'd completely misjudged the situation. Russell clearly had no such doubt.

"That's exactly what we think," Russell said. "Was anyone with you? Can anyone confirm that you were here all night?"

"No, I was here alone," Melville-Jones said, but Joe heard the hitch in his voice.

"All night?" he asked.

Melville-Jones shot him an angry look.

"I had a visitor at around eleven," Melville-Jones admitted. "But he didn't stay long."

Russell stood up and paced slowly across the room, fingers running along the spines of books in the shelf. A bead of sweat broke out on Melville-Jones's forehead.

"This visitor," Russell said, "it wasn't Chris, by any chance? What happened? Did you catch him going through your files looking for more secrets to share? Is that why you killed him? Is that it?"

"I think you should leave now," Melville-Jones said, standing up angrily. "If you have any further questions, I'd like to call my lawyer."

"We're asking politely, there's no need to get agitated."

"I'll have you in front of the Commissioner of Police," Melville-Jones spluttered.

"Oh, that won't help. We're not police, Mr Melville-Jones. I'm sorry if we gave you the wrong impression."

Melville-Jones's mouth opened in protest and then shut, dumbfounded.

"We just want to know what happened to our friend," Joe said. "We know you were paying him..."

"It wasn't like that," Melville-Jones hissed, sitting back down. "I wasn't paying for sex. We were in a relationship. I was only too happy to give him money if he needed it, but it wasn't in exchange for sex. I loved him and he loved me. At least, he said he did."

Russell had been about to throw out the next question, confirming their assumption that Melville-Jones had killed Chris, but this confession knocked him off his stride.

"A relationship?" he questioned.

"Yes," Melville-Jones insisted. "Well, as much as our clandestine meetings could ever be called a relationship. It wasn't like you're suggesting though. I wasn't paying him for sex, and nor was I paying him to keep quiet. I was happy to help him. Especially if it was to help his business. He was such a talented young man."

He smiled sadly at them. Russell turned to look at Joe, frowning. Had they got this so wrong? Another creeping thought was beginning to form in Russell's mind.

"Did you ever talk to Chris about your business?" Russell asked.

"God no," Melville-Jones laughed. "It would be bad enough for the constituents to discover their MP liked boys, let alone find out I'd been sharing government secrets. Even I'm not that stupid."

"I don't mean your work," Russell clarified. "I was talking about the family business."

"Oh that," Melville-Jones said dismissively. "Sometimes. But it would always lead to quarrels, so I tried to avoid it. He was cross because my brother was selling the corner house on Frith."

"And evicting the Campbell Centre," Joe snapped.

"I tried to stop the deal, but I really don't have a lot of say in it. The purchaser wanted vacant possession. My brother had already agreed."

"The purchaser being Tony Lagorio?"

"How did you know that?"

"He told me," Russell said. "And he also told me he'd been paying Chris to get information from you so he could drive down the price."

"Oh," Melville-Jones said, deflating more as the realisation sank in. "Oh, well that does explain a few things."

"What do you mean?"

"Well, Chris was cross about the charity, so I promised I'd help them find a new home. Anonymously, of course."

"Of course," Russell said.

"And that seemed to satisfy him for a while, but then recently he started bringing it up again. He kept going on about the money and how my family were corrupt and selfish. I thought it was because he was annoyed with Gavin. They were always falling out, those two. Nothing I could do about it, of course."

Joe noticed Russell freeze—another piece had just slotted into place.

"I got quite annoyed with him, if I'm honest," Melville-Jones continued. "After all, I'd promised him that my share of the money from the sale was going to fund my contribution to the new Campbell Centre, and the rest was going to him, indirectly, anyway. Gavin's father, my brother, had agreed to invest in their label."

"Yes," said Joe, bitterly. "But only on the condition that Chris was no longer involved."

"What?"

"Gavin was forcing him out. The lawyers—your family lawyers—had already issued the paperwork."

Melville-Jones slumped in his seat.

"Oh dear," was all he said.

"Thanks for your time, Mr Melville-Jones," Russell said abruptly. "You've been very helpful."

He turned to a rather surprised Joe.

"Come on, we've wasted enough time."

"WHERE THE HELL are we going?" Joe demanded.

One minute they'd been grilling a suspect, and the next, Russell was out of the blocks like a hare on a dog track. It was all Joe could do to keep up as they dashed across another pedestrian crossing, heading back towards Soho.

"What's going on?"

"I can't believe I've been so stupid," Russell said. "It was staring me in the face the whole time."

"What?" Joe asked. "Slow down a minute!"

"I know who killed Chris," Russell shouted as they dashed over the pedestrian crossing, heading back towards Soho.

"Who?" Joe called again.

"No time, come on."

Joe had always considered himself quite fit, but Russell could move extraordinarily fast for a portly man. As they dashed through the streets, Joe tried to piece everything together. How did the conversation they'd just had tie in with everything they had learned so far?

On the way to see Melville-Jones, Russell had been convinced that he was the one who'd killed Chris. Now, something the MP had said had lit a fire under Russell, and Joe was damned if he could figure it out.

"Wait here," Russell said. "And cover the side door. If he comes out, tackle him to the ground."

"Who?"

"Who do you think?"

Russell dashed away leaving Joe standing in the street. He looked up at the building Russell had gone into, and everything started to make sense.

The door to the studio—Chris and Gavin's studio—swung shut with a bang.

RUSSELL TOOK THE STAIRS two at a time, annoyed that he had missed the clues until now and angry that he had wasted time. The studio doors bounced off the wall as he slammed them open and stormed through.

The main gallery room was empty, but there was a light on in the small internal office. Good.

Gavin jumped back from the desk as Russell barged into the office. He dropped the overnight bag he'd been busy stuffing with paperwork.

"Going somewhere?" Russell asked.

"What are you doing here?" Gavin stammered.

"Why did you do it?" Russell fumed. "You could have started again with your own business, with your own designs. Why did you have to try to take all this from Chris?"

Gavin backed up, trying to put some distance between himself and Russell.

"I don't know what you're talking about. Get out, or I'll call the police."

Russell stopped, effectively blocking the door in case Gavin tried to make a run for it.

"You do that. It'll save me the effort. I'm sure they'd be very interested to hear how you killed Chris," he said.

"What?" Gavin spluttered, but Russell could see he'd got it right. Gavin was already looking for a way to get out.

"You were jealous of his popularity," he continued. "Jealous of his talent. You wanted to crush his dreams because he was better than you."

"That's not true," Gavin said defiantly. "The company used both of our designs, not just his."

"But none of yours were in the new line, that's why you went running to Daddy to get his lawyers to help you buy Chris out."

"No, I…"

"But then you realised that it wouldn't work, because your father would never expose his company to the kind of scandal that Chris had uncovered in your family. And you couldn't handle the fact that Chris would get to keep the business. You couldn't cope with the idea that his designs would be the backbone of the new line. You could already see his popularity outshining yours."

Gavin looked down, his head sagged. Russell had seen it many times before; when the defiance leaves the suspect and the truth comes out.

"He always got everything he wanted," Gavin said quietly. "He was the handsome one, the talented one, the confident and funny one. He had everything, and he knew it. When I first met him, I was besotted. Did you know that?"

"No," Russell didn't want to interrupt the train of thought.

"Well, I was. I just wanted to be near him. I knew he needed money to make the business work. That whole cooperative thing was just more people hanging on his shirt tails. He almost bit my hand off when I suggested we partner up. I was so happy that I would be the one to make his dream a reality."

Russell relaxed his position slightly, feeling that Gavin was less likely to try running if he was talking like this.

"And we didn't just form a business partnership either," Gavin said. "We started sleeping together. And because of the fool I am, I thought it was because he liked me. I should have known he was just using me to cashflow the business while he paid Tony back his stake."

He shook his head at the memory.

"I was an idiot. It took me too long to see what he was really like. Then suddenly he had all this money, but he wouldn't tell me where it was coming from. And he kept lying about where he had been, and who he had been with. It was his friend Paul that let it slip in the end. He'd followed him."

"To your uncle's house?"

Gavin nodded.

"Uncle Robert wouldn't believe me that Chris was just using him too. He said they were in love, and he was happy to give Chris any money he needed. When I tackled Chris about it, he just laughed at me."

So it *was* Chris's arrogance that got him killed, Russell thought.

"I told him I would buy him out. Pay him to go away quietly and leave us alone. My father agreed to give me the money. I even got our lawyers to draw up the documents. He would get nothing but cash out of the deal. Everything else would be mine."

"So what happened?"

"Chris flipped out. He said he'd go to the press with what he had. Said he had enough evidence of corruption and fraud, and God knows what else to ruin my whole family if I carried on with the lawyers. He had photographs of him and my uncle in bed together. Photographs he said he would give to the papers."

Gavin shuddered.

"So you killed him?"

"I didn't know what else to do. He was serious. He was going to share everything: the business deals, the backhanders, my uncle's sexuality. He would have destroyed all of us."

Gavin looked up at him, his eyes red-rimmed and angry.

"I followed him to the club. I knew Tony was itching to find him, because he'd been by the studio earlier. I guessed why Tony wanted to find him, and when he left the club I picked him up. I was going to try and talk some sense into him, pay him off... I don't know."

Gavin shook his head. Russell said nothing.

"I drove him to the flat. I promised to pay him double what Tony was offering for whatever evidence he had. But when we got there, he started taking the piss. He said even my uncle was better in bed than me. I lost it. I was so angry. Before I knew it, I'd killed him."

"You took the film from his camera?" Russell asked.

Gavin nodded.

"I thought that it was the evidence I was after, but it was just some pictures of him and his little mate, pissing about like schoolboys, getting ready to go out."

"So you came back yesterday to get everything else before it got back to Tony?" Russell had been wrong thinking it was Skinner who'd trashed the flat and hit Joe.

"Or you. I'm sorry. I knew you were digging for answers, and I didn't want either of you to find whatever he had. He abused my trust. He abused my uncle's trust, and I stood to lose everything if he carried on. He had his little crusade about the charity. He wanted my father to just donate the building to them. He always thought he could just have whatever he wanted."

Gavin picked up the holdall, shoved another sheaf of papers inside, zipped it up and hefted it onto his shoulder.

"I didn't mean to kill him," he said, sadly. "I loved him, once."

He went to walk past, but Russell put an arm out and stopped him.

"I can't let you go," Russell said.

"You're not in the police any more," Gavin hissed, pushing his hand away.

Russell grabbed his arm to hold him back, but Gavin slammed his head forward, smashing his forehead into the bridge of Russell's nose. As Russell let go, Gavin dashed past.

By the time Russell had regrouped enough to follow, Gavin was already hurtling down the stairs.

"Shit," Russell said, sprinting after him.

JOE HEARD RUSSELL'S warning shouts just as the side door banged open and Gavin ran out. He barely had time to react, but got his leg out in time to send Gavin sprawling across the pavement.

Joe pounced on him, a knee in his back, and pulled his arm up behind him so he couldn't twist out of his grip. Gavin bucked and struggled, so Joe punched him once, hard and quick to the side of the head.

Gavin slumped as Russell arrived, panting, with blood dripping from his nose.

"Who'd have thought you'd end up being the brawn of the team?"

And Joe smiled, because they were a team.

"I didn't grow up as the weedy, unpopular gay kid in my school without learning a few killer moves," he said.

8.

THE RED LION WAS heaving again, filled to the rafters with Chris's friends, all gathered to celebrate him, mourn him, share stories about him.

Russell, Joe and Paul were crammed in at a corner table, and hadn't had to pay for a single drink yet.

"Chris would have loved this," Paul said, smiling sadly.

Russell punched his arm.

"I thought we had a deal," he teased. "No sad faces. Anyway, you said you were going to do a turn for us."

"Later," Paul said. "Patty needs a few stiffeners before she gets her frock on."

"I bet she does," Russell laughed.

Paul raised a glass.

"To Chris," he said. "And to you two for catching his killer."

He pressed his open palms to his cheeks, fingers splayed—the perfect impression of a helpless damsel from a vintage film. "My heroes..." he cooed.

"Give over," Russell laughed.

"It's got to feel good, though, hasn't it?" Paul asked. "Being back in the saddle."

"Not as good as seeing the look on Skinner's face when we hauled Gavin into the station. Skinner's going to have some questions to answer himself now."

"And Tony's going to have to find himself another bent cop," Joe said.

"I shouldn't think he'll have much trouble with that," Russell said.

He fixed Paul with his sternest look. "And you, young man, are going to promise me that you'll stop extorting money from that poor MP."

"He's hardly poor," Paul sulked.

"No, but it's his life, and his secret to keep. Not everyone has the kind of freedom you kids do. Besides, he loved Chris. He's suffered just as much as the rest of us."

"Okay, fine," Paul said, rolling his eyes, though they all knew his huff was just for show.

As three more pints were delivered to the table, Joe looked up to see Luc smiling down at him.

"I hear you're a hero now," Luc said, slipping onto the bench beside him, and handing out the drinks.

Joe felt himself blush as Luc squeezed his thigh.

"I thought you were going back to Paris?" Joe asked.

"Paris can wait," Luc replied.

As Bowie's "Modern Love" came on the jukebox, Joe took Luc's hand in his, lacing their fingers together. He would always miss Chris, but he had his own life to lead now too.

TAINTED LOVE

BEFORE YOU GO

Dear Reader,

Thank you for reading the first in the Soho Noir series. I do hope you enjoyed it.

If you did, please leave a review in the place you bought the book from.

Reviews help authors like me to make sales, and break through the barriers to get their work seen. It's the best gift you can possibly give.

Thanks again for reading.

Yours,
T.S. Hunter

ABOUT THE AUTHOR

Claiming to be only half-Welsh, T.S. Hunter lived in South Wales for much of his latter teens, moving to London as soon as confidence and finances allowed. He never looked back.

He has variously been a teacher, a cocktail waiter, a podium dancer and a removal man, but his passion for writing has been the only constant.

He's a confident and engaging speaker and guest, who is as passionate about writing and storytelling as he is about promoting mainstream LGBT fiction.

He now lives with his husband in the country, and is active on social media as @TSHunter5.

TAINTED LOVE

Lightning Source UK Ltd.
Milton Keynes UK
UKHW042142070719
345743UK00001B/8/P